"I didn't want to come here."

"Nor I."

"I have to hold you." Robert's voice thickened, grew hoarse. "Do you understand?"

Maya nodded, past words, and flew into his arms, pressing her cheek to his chest. The regular, comforting beat of his heart quickened under her ear.

"I can't help how I feel," he whispered, and his lips covered hers. He pulled her closer, fitting her against him as the kiss deepened.

Eleven years had done nothing to diminish his power. Her body sizzled with the fiery message he sent to every cell in her body. No matter that a little warning voice in her head muttered that he wasn't for her—he was what she'd always wanted.

A man held her, not the boy she'd once known. Just as she was not a naive girl, but a woman who recognized her own unfulfilled need. For him.

He broke the kiss, but continued to hold her, his lips brushing hers.

"It's still there," he whispered, "still between us. We're damn well trapped."

Dear Reader,

Welcome to Silhouette **Special Edition** . . . welcome to romance. Each month Silhouette **Special Edition** publishes six novels with you in mind—stories of love and life, tales that you can identify with— romance with that little ''something special'' added in.

And this month is no exception to the rule. May 1991 brings *No Quarter Given* by Lindsay McKenna—the first in the thrilling WOMEN OF GLORY series. Don't miss more of this compelling collection coming in June and July. Stories by wonderful writers Curtiss Ann Matlock, Tracy Sinclair, Sherryl Woods, Diana Stuart and Lorraine Carroll (with her first **Special Edition!**) round out this merry month.

In each Silhouette **Special Edition**, we're dedicated to bringing you the romances that you dream about— the type of stories that delight as well as bring a tear to the eye. And that's what Silhouette **Special Edition** is all about—special books by special authors for special readers!

I hope you enjoy this book and all of the stories to come.

Sincerely,

Tara Gavin
Senior Editor

DIANA STUART
The Moon Pool

Silhouette Special Edition

Published by Silhouette Books New York

America's Publisher of Contemporary Romance

SILHOUETTE BOOKS
300 East 42nd St., New York, N.Y. 10017

THE MOON POOL

ISBN: 0-373-09671-2

First Silhouette Books printing May 1991

Books by Diana Stuart

Silhouette Desire

A Prime Specimen #172
Leader of the Pack #238
The Shadow Between #257

Silhouette Special Edition

Out of a Dream #353
The Moon Pool #671

DIANA STUART

presently lives in the Hudson River highlands. She is a registered nurse and has also been publishing Gothic and adventure romance novels since 1973. She is fascinated by Indian cultures. Diana is a native Californian.

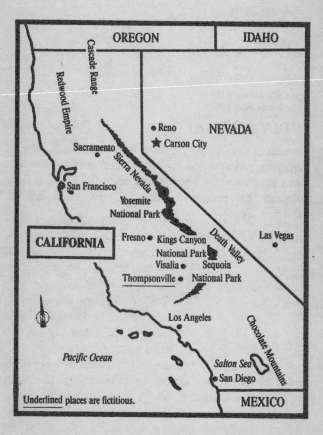

OREGON

IDAHO

Cascade Range

Redwood Empire

Reno

NEVADA

★ Carson City

Sacramento

Sierra Nevada

San Francisco

Yosemite
National Park

CALIFORNIA

Fresno ● Kings Canyon

Death Valley

Las Vegas

National Park

Visalia ●

Sequoia

Thompsonville ●

National Park

N

Los Angeles

Chocolate Mountains

Pacific Ocean

Salton Sea

San Diego

Underlined places are fictitious.

MEXICO

Chapter One

The night wind mixed the sweetness of orange blossoms with the green scent of riotous growth from the wild thickets along the stream swollen with snowmelt from the Sierras. Robert Pierson filled his lungs with the promise of spring and felt his tense muscles ease. This was reality—the caressing breeze, the moon-bright night, the miracle of the earth sprouting after the winter chill. For the moment he'd leave everything else behind and give himself up to this silver-washed May night.

When he'd left the house he hadn't been consciously aware of his destination but he'd found himself drawn to the farthest reaches of the grape ranch his great-grandfather had named Pierson's Pride. Here, among the pale trunks of the giant sycamores, was where his father had brought him over ten years ago, the night before Robert left for Stanford University. Of all the places his father could have chosen, this was the worst. Besides, it was too late for any rapport between them, but his father had insisted.

"Here I can forget myself," George Pierson told his son. "Here I'm a man without a name, I own nothing. Here I realize I'm only a part of all that exists and the knowledge brings me peace."

It was the first time Robert had understood his mother wasn't the only unhappy partner in his parents' marriage and he almost could forgive his father for the misery she'd suffered. Almost.

Now, at twenty-nine, Robert was no longer a child caught in the middle. Yet, though his father had been dead for three years, he still thought of the ranch and the house as belonging to George Pierson and being back at Pierson's Pride unsettled him. Why the hell hadn't his father left everything to his wife, Robert's mother, instead of merely willing her a life estate?

He knew I hated the place, Robert told himself. He wanted to force me to live here. He hasn't. Nothing and nobody ever will.

A frown furrowed his forehead. If it hadn't been for Joe Halago's call he wouldn't be at the ranch now. He'd be at home in his San Francisco condo instead of back in the San Joaquin Valley heading for a place that had haunted him for eleven years.

The past was better off forgotten. He'd come away from the house so he wouldn't remember, but this sycamore grove held a specter he'd prefer not to confront.

Robert paused beside a ghost-gray trunk and the chorus of frogs, which had fallen silent at his passing, rose again, their courting song shrill and insistent. Turn back? He shook his head. He couldn't bear to be shut up in his father's house. He needed the freedom of the night.

He'd have been wise to turn Joe down, but how could he when Joe's need was so acute? They'd been friends since their first year in medical school. Sometimes he thought Joe knew him better than he knew himself. He'd needed a vacation from his too-busy San Francisco practice anyway. Spending a couple of months as a replacement for Joe in the Thompsonville migrant workers' clinic might help bring back his enthusiasm for medicine.

Above the frogs' clamor he heard a splash from the stream that flowed through the grove. A trout jumping for a passing moth? No, too loud unless it was the primal ancestor of all trout. More likely some nocturnal animal fishing.

Curious, he eased toward the stream, stepping carefully to avoid making a noise that might frighten away whatever it was. Moonlight slanting between the trees turned the water to silver as it rushed between and over the banks. He saw no animals. Perhaps a rock, dislodged by the high water, had dropped into the stream. As he leaned against a tree, his eye was caught by eddies in a pool that had formed where huge boulders on the opposite bank trapped the overflow.

Suddenly water splashed in thousands of silver droplets as a sleek dark head broke through the surface of the pool. Robert, unmoving, held his breath as a vision rose before him—white shoulders, achingly beautiful breasts with erect nipples, the beginning flare of hips. She seemed so unreal that he found himself wondering if what still lay concealed under the water was a mermaid's tail.

With her body illuminated by moonlight but her face concealed by shadow, she threw back her head, raised her arms skyward and chanted words that were neither

English nor Spanish, words he didn't recognize, words with an ancient, primitive beat. He was spellbound, enchanted by her unearthly beauty.

He couldn't be hallucinating; she had to be real. Who was she? Why was she here? The answers could wait while he watched her, while he absorbed the vision of her into his entire being.

Her words were a paean to the night, to the moon, to nature. Listening, she made him believe she was the one who belonged here in the grove while he was but a trespasser.

Her voice slowed, stopped. With a motion so quick it startled him, she slapped the palms of her hands down sharply against the water, sending spray flying. One cool drop traveled across the stream to touch his lips, and when his tongue captured it he had the strange sensation he'd tasted a magic potion that would link him to her forever. An almost forgotten fragment of a poem came to him: *"La Belle Dame sans Merci/Hath thee in thrall...."*

Something like that, anyway. Keats, if he remembered correctly—it'd been a long time since English lit. The poem told of a beautiful but cruel enchantress who wasn't human. Obviously such creatures didn't exist. At the same time he couldn't bring himself to call across the water to her because it would break the spell.

At first he'd appreciated her as he would have any marvelous work of art, but his blood was beginning to pulse hot and fast with desire. He wanted her. Wanted desperately to possess her, to know what she knew, to be a part of her. To belong. Without realizing what he was doing, he reached his arms toward her and straightened from his leaning position, intent on finding a way to cross the surging stream separating them. He took a step and dried leaves crackled underfoot.

She held perfectly still for an instant, then turned abruptly, grasped a rock and levered herself from the water, her back to him. He caught a glimpse of a slim waist and round, taut buttocks before she glided into a cleft between two giant granite boulders and disappeared from view.

"Wait!" he called after her.

Too late.

If he plunged into the turbulent current, he ran the risk of being swept under. A few feet upstream, Robert found a fallen tree extending partway across the swollen waters, climbed onto it and leaped to the opposite bank. He searched but saw no sign of the dark-haired woman.

There wasn't a road to the grove; she must have walked here, as he had. He listened but could hear no crackling of ground debris to give him a clue to which way she'd gone. She had to be here somewhere. When she moved he'd find her. After a few moments, the muffled thud of a horse's hooves told him he was wrong and she was beyond his reach.

A sense of loss settled over him, as dank and gray as tule fog. He retraced his steps, climbed onto the rock where she'd stood and looked down at the pool where he'd seen her surface, reliving every second. If only the moonlight had touched her face clearly so he'd recognize her if he met her again. He smiled slightly, thinking he'd know the rest of her. A lot of good that did him unless he managed to undress every well-shaped dark-haired woman he came across. Fun but hardly practical.

Somehow he'd find her. Obeying an impulse he didn't understand, Robert stared into the shadows of the night

and shouted, "She's mine!" He flung the challenge at
the night, at the moon.

At her.

No one answered. Not even the frogs.

Maya Najero urged Padrino into a lope, wanting to
put as much distance as possible between her and her
unseen watcher. Though she'd heard only a rustle of dry
leaves, somehow she knew he was a man and not an animal. Who was he? Had he recognized her?

She thought not. After all, she'd been gone from the
San Joaquin Valley for nine years. Whatever had possessed her to come here tonight? True, she'd needed
privacy to chant the ancient Yaqui words her grandfather had taught her, needed the cleansing of the snowmelt waters and the healing rays of the moon, but this
place held bad memories, the worst of her life.

Perhaps she'd been drawn to the pool to exorcise those
ghosts from the past.

Once she thought she'd never return to the Valley,
never come home again. At the same time she knew she
belonged here and that she must come back someday.
Now it was safe to return—*he* was gone. He didn't live
in the Valley; she didn't have to worry about seeing him.

She liked San Diego well enough but it wasn't
Thompsonville. When her cousin Salvator Ramirez had
written to tell her Dr. Halago was looking for an R.N. to
run La Raza Clínica and asked if it wasn't time for her
to come home, she'd known Sal was right.

Her grandfather would have approved of her return.
"These are our people, yours and mine," he'd always
said. "You and I, we are healers of our people—never
forget."

She hadn't forgotten; she didn't regret her decision to return. Her heart had always been where she'd grown up.

But she'd been foolish to visit the moon pool. She wouldn't make that mistake again.

Chapter Two

At eight-thirty on Monday, Maya shut the door to her apartment and stepped into a morning scented by orange blossoms. She'd been lucky enough to rent the second floor of what must once have been the frame ranch house in an ancient Valencia and navel grove, so she was surrounded by orange trees—close to living in paradise. Taking a deep breath of the sweetened air, she smiled. It was good to be home.

Her landlady, Beatrice Reinholt, a widow in her sixties who lived downstairs, had left for a four-month visit to Australia two days after Maya moved in.

"I'm so glad to find someone responsible to rent the apartment to," Beatrice had told her. "I hated to leave the place empty. Feel free to pick all the oranges you like—some of last year's ripe Valencias are still on the trees."

Though she'd found Beatrice friendly enough, Maya liked the idea of having no one else living in the house. Even as a child she'd tended to be a loner.

Sliding into what she liked to think of as her "classic" VW bug, she drove along eucalyptus-lined roads to an old frame building on the eastern edge of town. When she was growing up in Thompsonville, this had been a Chicano bar—a cantina they called it—and it hadn't been new then. Now, repainted and reroofed, it housed La Raza Clínica.

She parked her car in back, locked it and looked for the employee's entrance. The only door she saw had no sign on its painted blue surface so she walked around to the main entrance in the front. The long, low and aging building was a far cry from the multistoried steel-and-glass hospital where she'd worked in San Diego.

But it housed the clinic. A Chicano clinic. In Thompsonville. The clinic had been no more than a dream of her people when she'd left the town at eighteen, vowing never to return. How many other things had changed for the better here in nine years? How many for the worse?

Being away from the San Joaquin Valley had taught her more than what she'd learned in her classes at the University of California. Her years at San Diego State University had given her a degree in nursing but she'd also found herself accepted for what she was—and it had nothing to do with whether she came from a Chicano grape picker's family or not.

Never mind her vow, it was time she came home. If nothing else, she owed something to the children growing up in Thompsonville, as she had. Like Joe Halago, M.D., she was a living example that proved Chicanos didn't have to be grape pickers. They could be doctors and nurses, could be anything they chose to be and had the ability to be. They were *not* second-class citizens.

Besides, her grandfather had expected her to return to Thompsonville; he'd expected her to replace him when he died. She was a nurse, not the healer Grandfather had been—no one could ever replace Caesar Gabaldon. Still, she'd do as much as she could for those who'd trusted him.

Her grandfather had expected her to come home.

When he interviewed her, she'd liked Joe Halago immediately and had looked forward to working with him. Unfortunately, Joe's bleeding gastric ulcer had laid him low, sending him to the Stanford Hospital operating room for surgery.

Happily he'd come through all right but he'd need a couple of months to convalesce. She wondered what kind of a doctor he'd found for a temporary replacement. Probably another Chicano. What doctor would tolerate the low fees at La Raza Clínica other than someone determined to help his own? Or, possibly, her own. It'd be really fine to work with a woman doctor.

As Maya opened the front door, she tried to decide what to call the receptionist. Mrs. Alvarado was her name but Joe had said everyone called her Angela. Would the receptionist resent a stranger using her first name? Or would she be put off by a more formal address?

Maya crossed the empty waiting room to reach the desk of the white-clad, plump, middle-aged woman. Mrs. Alvarado seemed startled to see her.

"I'm—" she began.

"*Dios!*" the woman exclaimed, a hand to her chest. "What a fright you gave me. I thought for a moment I was a girl again and Estella Gabaldon was walking toward me. I'd know you anywhere, Maya Najero—you're the image of your beautiful mother, God rest her soul.''

Maya couldn't remember her mother, who'd died when she was three, and the words warmed her, even though she'd often been told that she resembled her mother. But, from the few pictures she'd seen of Estella, Maya was convinced her mother had been far prettier than she was.

''Welcome to La Raza Clínica, Maya,'' the receptionist added, rising. ''I'm Angela.'' She came around the desk and embraced Maya.

As Maya returned her hug, she decided it was going to be a real pleasure to work here.

Robert parked his Italian sports coupe next to a bright red but elderly VW bug and strode to the blue door at the back of the old building.

''It's not much to look at from the outside,'' Joe had told him from his hospital bed at Stanford, ''but we're pretty well equipped, considering our never-quite-secure financial status. We're lucky as hell to get an internist of your caliber.''

''How could I refuse the guy who pulled me through neuroanatomy?'' Robert demanded, thinking they'd done the partial gastrectomy on Joe none too soon since his normally healthy brown skin was still a sickly gray. ''If you hadn't been my lab partner I wouldn't even be a doctor, much less an internist.''

So here he was back home, for better or worse—but not for long. And solely to help Joe out at the clinic. Perhaps he could also set up decent billing procedures during his locum—he was none too sure of Joe's financial ability. In either case, he was here to work at the clinic, not to take over at the ranch.

Pierson's Pride had survived without him since his father's death and would go on doing so, despite Salvator Ramirez's doubts about the new vineyard manager Robert's mother had hired.

He'd grown up with Sal and his old *compadre* made a first-class foreman, but Sal didn't seem to realize Robert had no interest in the ranch business. And never would have.

He opened the door, walked into the back of the clinic and stepped into Joe's small cubicle. Nothing like his spacious walnut-paneled San Francisco office but he hadn't expected anything fancy, and to tell the truth, he was glad it wasn't.

La Raza Clínica would get him back to the basics, to treating people with real medical problems. People who needed his skills. He was an internist, damn it, and tired of being a half-assed psychiatrist to wealthy middle-aged women with imagined ills and stressed workaholic men whose problems arose from life-styles they refused to change. His partner griped about being left to handle the office alone, but actually Bill was better suited to their practice than he was. They'd been looking for an associate and he hoped Bill would find one before he got back to take some of the pressure off.

If he didn't find his practice as interesting as it once had been, he also felt San Francisco itself wasn't as exciting as when he'd first moved to the city.

Not that Thompsonville had *ever* been exciting. Nor was it now—except for the naiad he'd surprised in the sycamore grove. He'd dreamed of her last night, the most erotic dream he'd had in years.

Robert shook his head. Dreams were fine for teenagers, but as an adult he preferred real women. If the water nymph from the pool lived in the area he'd find her one way or another. He couldn't fail to in so small a town. And when he found her . . .

Voices drifted along the corridor, reminding him why he was here. Time to meet his co-workers. Joe had said something about hiring a new nurse from San Diego, though he hadn't mentioned her name. That made one new nurse and one new doctor arriving at the same time. Luckily the receptionist, Angela Alvarado, had been with the clinic since its start two years ago. She'd know where everything was and who everyone was.

The only problem Robert anticipated concerned the local doctors. Joe had warned him it was impossible to get any of them to see clinic patients who had conditions that needed a specialist's consultation.

"Our esteemed colleagues in Thompsonville," Joe had explained, "want to be sure they're paid. *Pro bono* work isn't on their agendas."

Hell, I'm from Thompsonville, Robert thought. The local docs can't very well turn *me* down.

As he walked along the corridor he took in his new working quarters—three examining rooms, one minor surgery room complete with a none-too-new X-ray machine, a tiny lab and, to his surprise, a small employees' lounge.

"I heard someone come in the back," a woman said, just as he reached the half-open door at the end of the corridor. "It might be the new doctor."

"I'll go and look." Another female voice, one with a melodic pitch that fell easy on the ears.

The door opened all the way. Robert stopped, waiting. A pretty dark-haired woman in a white uniform stepped into the corridor and, seeing him, halted abruptly. She drew in her breath and stared at him incredulously.

He hadn't meant to startle her and he opened his mouth to say so. Before he got a single word out he recognized her and suddenly his entire world turned upside down.

Not her, anyone but her.

It can't be, Maya told herself, gaping at the lean and rangy blond man towering over her, his brown eyes widening in surprise. She hadn't seen Robert Pierson in eleven years, but she knew him at once. Though she'd forgotten he was so tall; he was at least a head taller than Sal. And she hadn't remembered how devastatingly attractive he was. Her heart pounded in panic.

Not him, anyone but him.

He was the last person in the world she'd expected to find as Joe's replacement and the last person in the world she wanted to work with.

How could she possibly remain at the clinic with *him* here?

She couldn't move, she could only stare at him, speechless. Robert stood motionless and silent, too, apparently as shocked as she was by the meeting. Hadn't he known she'd been hired?

As her mind began to function again, a horrible suspicion gripped her. The moon pool was on Pierson property—it could have been Robert watching her the other night. Had he seen her naked? She couldn't bear to think he might have. Obviously he knew who she was. Had he, if he was the watcher, recognized her that night. Involuntarily she crossed her arms over her breasts. Why, oh why, had she returned to the Valley?

Robert struggled to regain his wits. Damn it, why hadn't Joe told him who he'd hired as the new nurse? And why did she have to be so beautiful it hurt to look at her? Obviously Maya hadn't expected to see him and she was none too happy about it.

Joe, did you set this up? he wondered.

But Joe would have no reason. He didn't even know Robert Pierson and Maya Najero had ever met each other. Joe wasn't playing games. Fate was.

Robert gazed at her mountain cat's golden eyes set slightly aslant in her lovely face and a hunch snaked into his mind. The more he thought about it, the more certain he became. The moonlit nymph he'd watched and wanted had been Maya.

The god-awful truth was he still wanted her. Stunned as he was to come on her so unexpectedly here in the clinic, the compulsion to run his hands along her enticing curves, to taste the never-forgotten sweetness of her lips, was almost more than he could resist.

He'd thought he'd successfully pigeonholed the past— God knew he didn't relish those memories—but seeing her brought everything back, including how it felt to hold her in his arms, and he burned with unwelcome desire. He couldn't take his eyes from her.

He was dimly aware of raised voices in the waiting room, but not until Maya turned from him to look toward the open door did he snap out of his bemusement.

"Maya! Emergency!" a woman called.

Maya sprang toward the door and he followed on her heels.

A plump middle-aged woman in white thrust the limp body of an infant about six months old at Maya. From the dusky color of the face, it was obvious the baby wasn't breathing. Maya grabbed the child and ran into one of the examining rooms. By the time he reached her, she had the baby on the table and was thrusting her finger into its mouth, checking for a foreign object. She found none.

"I'll start manual CPR," he told her. "You set up the equipment."

He bent to breathe into the child's nose and mouth as Maya searched for what they needed—an ambu bag or whatever other breathing aid the clinic had on hand, a suction machine, oxygen, a naso-tracheal catheter. Angela Alvarado came in to help her.

"The mother told me the baby's been sick with a high fever," the receptionist said. "She was bringing him here when he had a convulsion and stopped breathing."

Maya set up the equipment on a stand beside the examination table and turned on the suction machine. Robert suctioned mucus from the baby's throat, then took the ambu bag and the child's mask she handed him and continued forced respiration for the child.

"Check the heart," he ordered.

Maya put on her stethoscope and listened to the infant's chest while keeping an eye on her watch. "One hundred and ninety, Doctor," she said after a minute. "Fair to poor quality, but no irregularity." She noticed the child was pinking up, the death blue fading from his face. Thank God.

"He's beginning to breathe on his own," Robert said after a few more minutes. He stopped pumping the ambu bag but continued the oxygen, watching the baby closely.

Maya looked around for Angela but the receptionist had evidently gone back to her desk. "Shall I bring the mother in?" she asked Robert.

He nodded. "I need a brief history from her and she needs to see that her baby's alive. We're going to have to admit this little guy to the hospital for tests and treatment.''

After the ambulance had come and gone, taking mother and child to the I. R. Thompson Community Hospital, Angela told Maya and Robert coffee was waiting in the lounge.

"Regular clinic hours don't begin till nine-thirty," she said. "You better take your break now 'cause you won't get another until after twelve. If then. This place gets to be a madhouse by noon."

Maya saw, to her surprise, it was only nine-fifteen. She would have sworn they'd spent more than an hour resuscitating that baby.

"What's your diagnosis?" she asked Robert as he held open the door to the lounge for her.

He shook his head. "I'll have to bone up on my peds. I haven't treated anyone under sixteen since I was an intern. The boy could have had an unusually severe fever-induced convulsion or it might be more serious, perhaps an encephalitis complicating a virus infection." He shrugged. "Or a dozen other things I can't quite remember. I'll know more after the results of the tests I've ordered are back. At least I hope so."

He followed her to the table, where freshly brewed coffee waited. Maya poured herself a cup, hesitated, then set the glass pot back on the warmer. He was perfectly capable of pouring his own.

With the table, a two-seater couch and two straight-backed chairs, the lounge was crowded. Or maybe it just seemed that way because Robert was in the room with her. She wished he'd left the door open. While they'd fought to make the baby breathe again, she hadn't thought about who he was or the past. She'd only been conscious that they were a doctor and nurse teaming up to help a patient.

But now that the emergency was over and they were shut in this small room together, uneasiness tensed her muscles. He was more than the doctor she had to work with for the next few months, he was Robert Pierson, and it would be dangerous to forget that fact.

She perched herself on the edge of a straight chair and watched him stir sugar into his coffee, then carry it to the settee and sit down, setting his right foot casually across his left knee. He wore tan chinos and a tobacco-brown shirt under a tan silk jacket. Clothes had never dominated Robert. Nothing dominated him. It irritated her that he seemed so at ease.

She sipped her coffee and said nothing. He didn't speak either, and the silence stretched thinner and thinner until the click of the wall clock's minute hand moving a notch made her jump.

Robert had never been so acutely aware of a woman in his life. All his senses were on alert, focused to catch her every nuance. A faint scent of honeysuckle wafted to him when she lifted her cup to take a sip of coffee. Her scent, the same scent he remembered. Indescribably enticing.

As his glance took in the soft swell of her breasts under the white uniform, his fingers tingled with the need to touch her. He wanted her. He'd wanted her eleven years ago and he discovered now his desire for her hadn't ebbed in the time they'd been separated. He resented her, the past disturbed him, but that didn't lessen his need for her.

Her name was still Najero. Did that mean she wasn't married? Not necessarily. He clenched his jaw at the vision of Maya in another man's bed.

"Are you married?" he demanded.

Maya blinked, obviously startled by his question. "No." The frost edging the word implied it was really none of his business.

Then there wasn't one damn reason in the world to keep him from her. She was no innocent teenager now, she was an experienced woman. What had flared between them eleven years ago had gone unconsummated far too long. Unfinished business. He wasn't sure he liked her, he didn't trust her, but he'd never in his life desired any woman more. He meant to have her and do away with the haunted past once and for all.

The fiery glint in Robert's brown eyes made Maya grip her mug so hard her fingers whitened. His were lying eyes, their velvety softness giving no hint of the cruelty they hid. He made her incredibly nervous, staring at her like that. Yet it was more than nervousness that stole her breath and tripled her pulse rate. She was appalled to realize he had the ability to affect her like this despite the past. Despite the fact she loathed him.

The attraction electrifying the air between them was more potent, more compelling, than anything she'd ever felt for another man. She knew his fair hair would be silk under her fingers, knew how the insistent demand of his lips would increase her own throbbing need. She knew from experience. A bitter experience that had tainted her life, an experience she'd never risk repeating.

Maya tore her gaze from his mouth, the beautiful sensual mouth that had loved and hurt her. Never again!

She took a deep breath, let it out slowly and rose. "I'd like to take a quick look around before we start seeing patients," she said, amazed at how cool and calm she sounded.

He got to his feet, his body blocking her exit. "Is that your VW bug in back?" he asked.

She nodded.

"Strange—I once thought of you as the type who'd go for a foreign sports car," he said.

Maya's control snapped. "You don't have the slightest idea what I'm like! You never did and you don't now. Please move so I can get past."

"You're a beautiful woman, Maya." He flung the words at her as though they were poison darts.

She took a step back, dismayed, and suddenly recalled the watcher in the grove, a watcher she feared had been Robert. Her face flamed. Damn him! And damn the awareness that flamed through her from his nearness.

"I'd appreciate it if you remembered why we're at the clinic, Dr. Pierson." Maya spoke through clenched teeth. "I'd never have accepted the position if I'd known you were substituting for Dr. Halago, and, now that I find you are, I'm certainly tempted to walk out of here and never return."

"But you won't."

His smugness infuriated her. "If I can find a replacement I intend to do just that."

He held up his hand, palm toward her. "Joe'll have a relapse if you leave."

She bit her lip. Though she knew very well Robert was trying to con her, he did have a point. How could she walk out on a sick man? Or on her own people. After all, the clinic was for them.

How she wished Joe Halago's ulcer hadn't incapacitated him, that Joe was here instead of Robert. She knew that she and Joe would have worked well together. How in God's name could she work with Robert? If she stayed, and she felt she *had* to stay, somehow she must learn to tolerate him.

"If you'd behave professionally there'd be less of a problem," she snapped.

Robert's dark gaze trapped her, preventing her from moving. For a long, breathless moment she thought he meant to touch her.

"I'll give it a try," he said finally, and moved aside so she could leave the lounge.

Maya hurried along the corridor, angrier at herself than at him. If ever a man deserved to be hated, Robert Pierson did. She detested him, yet she'd let him get the upper hand in the lounge. For the last time.

She'd been naive at sixteen, in marked contrast to his eighteen-year-old prep school know-how. Not any longer. She'd learned a lot in eleven years and not all of it from books. He'd taken her by surprise today and, in her shock, she'd let him overwhelm her. But forewarned was forearmed.

He'd said it wouldn't happen again. Or had he? Certainly he'd made no promises. And even if he had, any promise of Robert's was worth less than a Tijuana centavo.

As for her reaction to him—okay, so he was sexy. So what? Sexy wasn't everything. In fact, it was nothing compared to honesty and kindness, words Robert didn't know the meaning of.

She didn't want any part of Robert Pierson and she'd make damn sure he knew it. The sooner he understood how she felt, the better.

Maya opened the door to the waiting room, already beginning to fill up, and Angela Alvarado beckoned her to the desk.

"Isn't Dr. Pierson a doll?" Angela whispered to her. "And single! He makes me wish I was ten—no, make that fifteen—years younger." She rolled her expressive brown eyes at Maya. "Lucky you, young enough and pretty on top of it."

"I wouldn't have him if he were the last man on earth!" Maya spoke so vehemently Angela gaped at her.

To her dismay, Maya noticed that the woman seated in the chair nearest the desk had overheard and was staring at her. When the woman's gaze shifted to the open doorway, Maya looked in that direction and saw Robert standing there watching her, his smile a challenge.

Her chin came up. Challenge accepted.

If Robert Pierson expected to find her the same dreamy adolescent she'd once been, he'd discover his mistake in a hurry. If he expected her to fall into his arms, he was way off course. If he expected anything at all from her besides medical competence when they worked together, he'd be disappointed. And it served him right. She relished the idea of a disappointed, misdirected, frustrated Robert.

This time, unlike eleven years ago, she was damned if she'd come out the loser.

Chapter Three

On Thursday evening, Maya hummed as she chopped vegetables for her evening meal while an orange-blossom-scented breeze teased the blue-and-white curtains at the open kitchen window. She'd picked ripe oranges off the surrounding trees this morning, something she hadn't done since she left Thompsonville.

She'd been away too long. Luckily the complication of Robert Pierson's presence at the clinic was temporary, because this was where she belonged.

Nothing tasted quite so good, tart and sweet at the same time, as a freshly picked orange. Or apricot. Or peach. Store-bought fruit never had the same tang. She loved this valley where she'd grown up.

"Take pleasure in everything the earth has to offer," her grandfather had often told her. "It is the greatest gift of all. Take what you need and then return the gift in your own way. Replenish."

She was trying.

The doorbell rang. Maya froze. She wasn't expecting anyone.

Unaware that she still held a paring knife in one hand, she walked slowly to the door, fighting down panic. It couldn't be Robert. He didn't know where she lived.

The clinic, though, had her address. He might have looked it up in the files. But why would he? After that disastrous first meeting at the clinic, she'd made it clear there'd be nothing between them except their professional relationship, and the next few days had gone quite smoothly. Because they worked well together didn't mean he had the right to expect anything more.

Taking a deep breath, she eased open the door.

"Hola, mi prima," the dark, stocky man standing there said. "Hi, cousin, how's it going?"

Her breath whooshed out in relief. "Sal! Come in."

He raised his eyebrows. "Who were you expecting?" He nodded at the knife she was carrying.

Maya flushed. "No one. I was cutting up carrots."

He followed her to the kitchen, glancing around as he passed through the living room. "You've got the place looking great. I like those Aztec prints."

"Not Aztec. Yaqui."

Sal shrugged. "You're the expert."

"Not really, I'm just an amateur collector. I got interested in the Yaquis because of my grandfather."

"A great old man. We lost a real healer when Caesar Gabaldon died."

She nodded. "He's why I went into nursing. How about a cup of coffee? Or join me for supper—if you like salad."

"Thanks, but I can't stay. Just dropped by for a minute."

Something in the tone of his voice alerted Maya. She laid the knife on the counter and confronted him. "Is this visit purely social or have you come loaded with cousinly advice?"

"Both." He shifted his shoulders, his dark brown eyes wary. "Don't take me wrong. I'm not trying to interfere. I know you're uptight 'cause Rob Pierson's working at the clinic with you. And I know you don't like him 'cause something went wrong between the two of you a long time ago. Whatever it was is your business and his, no?"

"It's between the two of us, yes. I don't care to discuss the past." She spoke more curtly than she intended. Sal was a friend, not an enemy. He was a steady man. Loyal and dependable. A man you could trust. Unlike Robert.

"Yeah, I understand," he said.

He didn't. No one could.

She glanced at Sal appraisingly. With his longish curly black hair and his athletic build, he looked younger than his thirty-two years. His frown sat uneasily on a broad, pleasant face more used to smiling.

"Rob and me go way back," he said. "Only three years' difference between us. I was the one taught him to ride, taught him a lot 'cause his father didn't have the time. He taught me stuff, too. Out of books, like that. When we were kids, Rob and me, we were *compadres,* you know?"

"What does this have to do with me?"

He crossed his arms over his broad chest. "I'm the only family you have left, Maya, otherwise I'd keep my mouth shut. What it is, Rob's been asking me questions, like do you ride Padrino sometimes. He makes it sound casual as hell but he forgets how well I know him.

The more offhand he sounds, the more interested he is. But what can I do? I tell him, sure, you took my horse the other evening, and he grins at me, happy as a gopher in a bean patch. I'm willing to mind my own business, but if I'm in danger of getting caught in the middle I want to know what's going on."

"Nothing's going on." Maya's voice was emphatic. "Not between Robert and me. Not between a Pierson and a Najero—especially a Najero whose mother was a Gabaldon." Her lip curled. "The Valley may be changing, Sal, but not *that* fast. And even if it were, I'm the last person in the world to get involved with a Pierson."

He muttered something that sounded like "That's what I keep telling her," but when she asked him to repeat the words more clearly, he shook his head.

"Doesn't have anything to do with you." He gazed at her unhappily and raked his fingers through his hair. "You remember I'm around anytime you want to talk, okay?"

"Gracias, primo." She managed a smile, since it wasn't Sal's fault Robert was asking him questions. "And thanks for letting me ride Padrino. I'd almost forgotten how great it is to be on a horse."

Sal opened his mouth, then shut it without saying anything. She knew he wanted to ask her where she'd ridden Padrino and what Robert had to do with the ride.

Not that she'd tell him if he did ask. How could she admit she'd bathed nude in the moon pool and been surprised by a hidden watcher? A watcher she was now certain had to be Robert. It sent angry shivers up her spine to think Robert had seen her unclad.

"Everything okay at the clinic?" Sal said at last.

She was grateful for the change of subject. "I can't believe how busy that place is. I thought we'd be seeing just Chicanos but all kinds of people come there—Anglos, blacks, Asians. All kinds of poor people. What did they do before La Raza Clínica opened?"

"Some of them died." Sal's voice was matter-of-fact. "Rob's the one keeping the clinic open until Joe gets on his feet again. None of the local docs will come near the place and Rob sure as hell's not working there for the money—think about it."

"I have no complaints about his ability as a doctor." She couldn't help the chill in her voice.

Sal shrugged. "People change. I'm not the same as I was ten years ago. Neither are you. Or Rob." He picked up a carrot round and popped it in his mouth. "Going to La Raza Clínica third-anniversary celebration next week?"

Maya smiled, glad he'd changed the subject. "If you'll come with me."

"You mean you haven't got a date?" He shook his head. "The guys around here must be blind."

"I've been too busy to meet anyone except patients. Besides, I'd rather go with you." She drew in her breath. "Oh, Sal, I'm sorry, I never thought I might be putting you on the spot. You probably have plans already."

"No. I've been too busy to meet anyone except grapevines."

Maya laughed at his echo of her words. "Come on, I know better. You've broken at least half of the female hearts in Thompsonville."

"I'll pick you up next Friday night, then," he said, surprising her by ignoring her teasing. "Don't forget costumes are the custom."

She made a face. "Costumes aren't my favorite thing."

"Humor us out-in-the-tules folk." He sighed. "I've got to get back to the ranch. I swear that damn manager Mrs. Pierson hired never saw a grape before, much less the vines they grow on. He's trouble waiting to happen. Sometimes I think I'm the only one who cares what goes on out there."

"Why *do* you care so much? It's not your ranch."

"I kind of feel like it is, in a way." Sal grinned at her. "*Poco loco,* that's me."

"A little crazy? I'd say *mucho loco*. If you and Robert are such good friends, why didn't he make you manager instead of this incompetent?"

"Maybe you don't know how old Mr. Pierson's will left his wife the right to live at the ranch house the rest of her life. With Rob living up in Frisco, he lets his mother make the decisions. When old Nat Gramercy took his boots off for the last time, Mrs. Pierson picked the new manager. 'Cause she liked his looks, I think. I can't find any other reason."

George Pierson had been Maya's friend; he'd filled the void in her life left by her dead father. But all she knew of his will was that he'd bequeathed her six thousand dollars. She'd bought the VW bug with it.

"Who actually owns Pierson's Pride now?" she asked.

"Rob and Laura, joint ownership. Rob's busy. He told me once he was like me—too busy to even think about getting married. And you can't expect Laura to take on the ranch. She's only eighteen and going off to college this fall."

Maya hadn't forgotten Robert had a younger sister but, since she'd never really known Laura, she hadn't thought about her in years.

"And none too soon," Sal muttered. "I'm gone," he added, striding toward the door.

Maya frowned as she watched him leave. What had he meant by that "none too soon" business? Laura's leaving in the fall was none too soon? Why? It didn't make sense. Was Laura a problem teen? On drugs? Surely it wasn't connected with Sal in any way.

Nothing a Pierson does is any of my business, Maya told herself firmly. Not unless they infringe on *my* rights.

She retrieved the paring knife and picked up a carrot. So Robert was too busy to get married. Not that she cared.

No matter what Sal said about people changing with the passage of time, it was strange how little Robert had changed physically. His face had lost is boyishness, that long lean frame had filled in some, but she'd have known him anywhere. Blond hair—golden, really—thick and straight, eyes the color of milk chocolate, lean face, all planes and angles. Lips with tender curves that belied the harsh lines of his face.

When she was sixteen, she'd thought he was the best-looking male she'd ever seen. When she was sixteen she'd thought she was in heaven when Robert noticed her. But what had happened then was more like hell....

Enough of the past! Maya decapitated a carrot with such violence the top end skipped across the counter and onto the floor.

On Friday, Robert stumbled through the back door to the clinic at nine, still half-asleep. Randy Mills, the baby he'd admitted to the hospital on Monday, had gone sour around midnight and he'd spent the rest of the night fighting to keep the boy alive. It wasn't until six this morning that he'd felt Randy might make it.

Whether Randy's doctor would make it through the day was another story. Maybe a cup of Angela's coffee would help. She made a hell of a lot better coffee than the machine at the hospital.

He passed an examining room and paused when he noticed Maya inside, setting out clean equipment. She glanced up and saw him.

"Good morning, Dr. Pierson," she said coolly.

From the way she spoke anyone would think they were strangers. Whatever else could be said about what had happened between them, they damn well weren't strangers, but he was too tired to challenge her this morning.

"You look exhausted," she added, her voice a trifle warmer. "Emergency call?"

"Randy."

Her eyes widened in alarm and she stepped closer to him. Close enough so he got an enticing whiff of honeysuckle.

"Is Randy all right?" she asked.

"He's stable. For the moment. I finally got a diagnosis from the tests. He's got Western equine encephalitis, complicated by bacterial pneumonia. The pneumonia organism's sensitive to half a dozen antibiotics. The encephalitis—" He let his words trail off.

Robert knew Maya was well aware there was no treatment for the arbovirus causing the equine encephalitis. Either Randy's immune system would be strong enough to overcome the bug or the boy would die.

"I never even looked for mosquito bites," she said after a moment. "I should have."

"He had bites on his legs. I saw them at the hospital. But don't feel bad—I ignored the bites, too. I'd considered encephalitis secondary to a virus infection but for some reason I didn't think of equine encephalitis. Stupid."

Mosquitoes carried the virus from bird to horse and then to man. In the San Joaquin Valley, with its many horses and heavy irrigation providing the water that attracted both mosquitoes and red-winged blackbirds, Western equine encephalitis was endemic. As he well knew. It should have been one of his tentative diagnoses from the moment he first saw Randy. Especially since children under a year of age were the most common victims.

"I never had a patient with it in San Diego," Maya said. "Have you ever seen a case in San Francisco?"

He smiled wryly. "Not a chance. My patients don't get bitten by mosquitoes."

Her lips quivered and he thought for a moment she was actually going to smile back. Instead she said, "I hate to tell you, but the waiting room is already full. I've isolated one patient and her mother in there." She nodded toward the closed door to an examining room across the hall. "Looks to me like chicken pox with superimposed staph or strep infection of some of the lesions."

Robert sighed. "I'd better see her pronto. When I finish, send them out the back door. Otherwise she'll shed varicella virus all over the waiting room when she walks through and infect every kid in the place."

Maya nodded and stepped past him to open the door. He followed her into the room and another clinic day began.

They were so busy that at one o'clock Angela took up a collection and sent her part-time assistant, Pat, out for pizza and sodas. If she hadn't, none of them would have had any lunch.

At six-fifteen the last patient left and Robert collapsed in his office. He needed a few minutes' rest before he could work up enough energy to make it to his car. He'd seen everything from gout to impending right heart failure. And he still had to check Randy and Pablo Hernandez, the heart patient, at the hospital. If Joe's days had been as frenetic as this, no wonder he'd developed a bleeding ulcer severe enough to require surgery.

Yet, tired as he was, Robert had a sense of satisfaction he hadn't felt since his internal medicine residency. He'd helped people who really needed him. He put his feet on the desk, tipped the chair back and closed his eyes.

Maya paused with her hand on the knob of the back door. The clinic was locked, Angela and Pat were gone. There was no reason for her not to go, too. Except that she hated to leave Robert asleep in his chair. He was exhausted and might well sleep for hours.

Though he needed the rest, she knew he wasn't through for the day—he still had hospital rounds to make. Should she wake him so he could finish what he had to do and go home to bed?

Robert Pierson's none of your business, she reminded herself.

True, but unfortunately, as the clinic nurse, she felt *Dr.* Pierson was.

Retracing her steps, she peered through the partly open office door. He was still asleep. She eased through the door and walked to his side. Judging by the blond stubble on his cheeks and chin, he hadn't had time to shave this morning. How harmlessly boyish he looked with those wicked brown eyes closed. His face, relaxed in sleep, seemed as young as when he'd been eighteen. For some reason, seeing him so defenseless tugged at her heart.

She'd known who he was ever since she could remember. Robert Pierson, the golden-haired boy who trailed her cousin Sal everywhere. By the time she was six, she knew that, unlike Sal, Robert didn't have to work at the ranch unless he wanted to because Robert was a Pierson.

He fascinated her so she watched him whenever she had the chance. By the time she was eight, she knew she wasn't ever supposed to talk to him or bother him. That was the year she'd met Robert's father for the first time when he bought her an ice-cream cone.

She'd been warned by her grandfather never to take anything from people she didn't know, but she did know George Pierson by sight. He was the *patrón,* the boss. All the workers' kids recognized him. When her grandfather came back to the truck, saw her eating the cone and found out where she had gotten it, he'd looked sad rather than angry. She hadn't found out what made him sad until years later.

The ice-cream cone had been the beginning of her friendship with George Pierson, a friendship that had enriched her life and also given her the chance to realize her potential. George had been a kind, patient and understanding man. The only characteristic Robert shared with his father was their brown eyes. Otherwise Robert was his mother's son, blond and tall and beautiful. And treacherous.

Remember that, she warned herself. Never mind how innocent he looks when he's asleep.

Maya reached to touch his shoulder to rouse him. She gasped with alarm when Robert's feet came off the desk, the chair swung around and his hand caught her wrist, pulling her toward him. For a moment, off balance, she feared she would land in his lap, but by grabbing the back of his chair, she managed to stay on her feet.

He rose, still holding her wrist, and she edged nervously away, tugging against his grasp. To her surprise, he let her go. Her wrist tingled where he'd touched her, the tingle spreading through her. Watching him warily, she caressed her wrist with her other hand until she realized what she was doing and stopped abruptly.

Aware she couldn't reach the door without brushing past him and hesitating to come that close, Maya decided to behave as though nothing unusual had happened.

"I came in to wake you up before I left," she said, hoping her voice didn't reveal her breathlessness. Next time he could sleep in his chair the entire night for all she cared.

"I knew you were standing beside me," he told her. "The smell of honeysuckle puts me on red alert."

He meant her cologne, she realized. She wore such a small amount she was amazed any of the scent still clung to her at the end of the day. A long, hard day.

"It's time to go home," she said firmly, trying in vain not to meet his gaze. If only he wasn't standing so close to her she could think more clearly.

"I've never been able to forget that scent," he murmured. "Or you."

She refused to be drawn into the past. Deliberately, she glanced at her watch.

"If you'd come by the hospital with me," he said, "we could have dinner together afterward."

His nearness really did unnerve her. Raising her eyebrows in what she hoped looked like cool amusement, at the same time she struggled to keep her voice from quavering. "I'm afraid dinner's not included in my professional duties, Doctor."

"I've been behaving, damn it! You can't deny I have." He rested his hand on her upper arm. "Can you?"

As the exciting warmth of his touch penetrated the cloth of her uniform sleeve, Maya realized with dismay that she felt a strong urge to lean toward him.

"I thought we agreed to avoid the personal." Maya forced herself to step back as she spoke and found she was in a corner. But at least his hand had dropped from her arm.

Why did she have to notice how strands of his chest hair curled in the vee of his blue shirt? And why should she find the sight erotic? As a nurse she'd seen scores of male patients' bodies and never once had their chest hair interested her in the slightest.

"We can't run away from what's between us," he said. "You know that as well as I do."

Much as she hated to admit it to herself, Robert still had the power to speed her pulse and stir her desire. But she'd die before she'd tell him so. He was her enemy and she'd be a fool to forget it.

"Do you have any idea how difficult it is to be alone with you and not touch you?" he demanded.

"All the more reason not to see each other off duty," she said. "If you'll please move, I really would like to go home."

He smiled one-sidedly. "I have you pretty well cornered, don't I?" He ran a hand along his stubbled jaw. "I wish I were a bit more presentable at the moment."

"Your appearance has nothing to do with my having or not having dinner with you," she snapped, angry at herself because she found his unshaven face sexy. Everything about this damn man was sexy! "I'd refuse even if you wore a white tie and tails. Just let me past and forget dinner."

He stepped closer, bending his head until she felt the warmth of his breath against her mouth when he spoke. "The trouble is I can't forget *you*."

Without touching her otherwise, he brushed his lips lightly over hers, sending a frisson of need deep within her. He eased away, his gaze questioning. Confused and shaken, she had no idea what he read in her eyes.

He nodded, apparently to himself. "We'll have dinner another time. When I'm not dead on my feet."

He edged sideways, leaning against his chair to allow her passage.

As she passed his desk, the phone rang, the shrill jangle startling her. Robert picked it up on the second ring.

"Dr. Pierson here."

Maya, at the door, hesitated. If this was an emergency call, he might need help.

"Is the eye bleeding?" Robert asked.

She tensed. Eye injuries were always serious.

After a moment of listening, Robert said, "No, don't bring him here, take him to the emergency room at the hospital. I'll meet you there." He set the phone down, looked up and seemed surprised to see her still there.

"I thought you might need me," she explained.

He grinned. "Professionally, no. Personally, yes. Shall I count the ways?"

"Good night!" she cried, and fled.

As she slid into the VW she warned herself she'd have to watch her step with Robert very, very carefully. Any road she traveled with him not only would be strewn with pitfalls but would be a dead end.

Hadn't she learned *anything* in eleven years?

Chapter Four

On Friday evening, Maya dressed for the clinic party, wondering if Robert would bother to show up. Sal had said few Anglos did. She'd be just as happy if Robert stayed home. Seeing him every day in the clinic was all she could handle.

When Sal rang the bell she opened her door and blinked in surprise at how he was dressed. "You said costumes, not fancy dress," she protested. "You're so loaded down with silver I don't know how you can move. We'll be some pair, a Californio don escorting a barefoot *pelada.*"

Sal entered the apartment, his gaze taking in what she wore. "You don't look all that raggedy to me, cousin. And I seem to see sandals on your feet."

Maya waved a hand. "I spoke figuratively. You are one handsome caballero in that black-and-silver outfit. Is it genuine?"

"Yeah. Passed down as a keepsake on my father's side. For the last eighty years no one's had the nerve to wear it—but why not? Why should possessions outlast people?"

Maya's fingers caressed the silver bracelet on her left wrist, unconsciously stroking the incised markings representing a snake's scales. "You have a point, Don Salvator."

Sal bowed slightly. "Your costume, *señorita,* will certainly pop a few eyeballs."

Maya glanced down at herself, at the white, low-necked chemise top with its bright yellow vest and the scarlet, black and yellow midcalf skirt. "It's a Poblana peasant's dress I bought in Mexico City a few years ago. I've never worn it before." She tugged at the neckline. "I didn't realize I'd be quite so exposed."

Sal raised his eyebrows. "Am I hearing right? This from the six-year-old brat who used to defy old Caesar by skinny-dipping in Ría Luna?"

Maya's flush had nothing to do with her childish escapades. She hoped Sal would never find out who'd caught her skinny-dipping in Moon Creek only a few short weeks ago.

"I guess I did give Grandfather a hard time," she said hastily. "Raising me couldn't have been easy for him."

"After your mother died, he fought off every attempt by others to take you away from him. My own mother wanted to bring you home but she, like the other women, was a little afraid of the old man."

"Of Grandfather? He was a healer, a *curandero.* He'd never hurt anyone."

Sal shrugged. "There are always those who believe curing and witchcraft go side by side."

"My grandfather was no *brujo,* no witch!" Maya's voice was indignant.

"Hey, you don't have to convince me. I'm on your side. Haven't I always been?"

Recalling some of the childhood scrapes Sal had helped her survive, Maya nodded. She had to admit her behavior hadn't been especially ladylike—but Sal had never told on her.

Once they were seated in Sal's pickup, on their way into town, he spoke again of her grandfather. "Since you healed Connie Olvera," he said, "they've been calling you *La Curandera.* They say you take after old Caesar."

"I'm a nurse, not a *curandera,*" Maya protested.

Concepción Olvera, screaming at the top of her voice that she was going blind, had arrived at the clinic last week escorted by a throng of agitated relatives.

Maya led her to an examining room, sat her down, shooed everyone out, then stood behind Connie's chair and put her hands over the young teenager's eyes, forcing Connie to close them. In a matter of minutes the girl quieted.

When Robert came in to examine her, Connie's vision was already returning. Apparently she'd either suffered temporary hysterical blindness or had a negative scotoma—where the center of vision is blocked temporarily by an area of blackness. Luckily for Connie, neither condition would result in permanent loss of vision.

"Connie's convinced everyone you healed her with your hands," Sal said.

Maya shook her head. "While I do believe there can be healing power in the laying on of hands, in Connie's case all I did was calm her down until time solved the problem."

"Whatever you did enhanced your reputation."

She slanted him a stern look. "Don't you dare encourage people to think I take after my grandfather."

"Just reporting what I hear, cuz." He pulled in behind parked cars along a side street several blocks from the clinic.

In the shadowed early evening, they joined others walking toward the sound of music and laughter coming from the clinic's parking lot. The spicy aroma of barbecued beef mingled with the heavy sweetness of night-blooming jasmine climbing an adobe wall. An orange cat parading along the top of the wall paused to bat at a white-winged moth, missed and almost fell. Regaining its balance the cat stalked on, tail held high, disclaiming any possible interest in moths.

Sal's steps faltered for a moment and he muttered under his breath.

"I didn't hear you," Maya said.

"Not important."

Aware something across the street had caught his attention, she followed his gaze. Robert's metallic blue Italian sports coupe was parked opposite them. Robert stood beside it, smiling down at a young blond woman.

Maya's heart contracted. She tried to look away and failed. Though Robert wasn't in costume, the woman wore a long skirt, a lace mantilla, and carried a fan. Her laughter, light and melodious, rang mockingly in Maya's ears. Forcing her attention from the pair, Maya marched stiffly on, assuring herself it made little difference to her who Robert escorted to the party. Or anywhere.

She could hardly believe she'd uttered the words when she heard herself ask, "Who's that with Dr. Pierson, Sal?"

"Don't you recognize Laura?"

The heaviness inside Maya's chest lifted. Laura. Robert's sister. He'd brought his sister.

"The last time I saw Laura she was a little girl."

"She's still a kid. Got a lot of growing up to do." Sal's voice was curt.

Maya glanced at him with raised eyebrows but he'd turned away to greet friends, who joined them. Swept along with the group, Maya lost sight of Robert and Laura.

The clinic parking lot overflowed with laughing, talking, eating, drinking people. Some daring souls even tried to dance to the music the band at the far end played. Sal introduced her around and everyone she met smiled and spoke to her pleasantly enough.

Eventually, though, she realized none of them, even those she'd known in the past, were fully at ease with her. Since she knew Chicanos normally were warm, friendly people, she decided the fault lay with her. Was she being too aloof? Or was it more intangible, something to do with what Sal had told her? Maybe he'd repeated the *curandera* gossip as a warning that she'd be treated differently, more cautiously. As her grandfather had been. Never excluded, but not quite included, either.

I'm just me, she wanted to tell them. Maya Najero. One of you.

But if that was true, why did she feel so alone?

Robert drifted through the crowd, absently admiring the colorful costumes, speaking to those he knew, all the while telling himself he was not here to watch Maya. What did it matter that she'd come with Sal? After all, Sal's mother and Maya's father had been brother and sister. Sal was her cousin. A relative. More importantly, Sal was an old friend, someone he trusted.

It meant nothing to him that Sal's arm encircled her shoulders as he guided her from one group to another, or that she smiled up at Sal far more freely than she ever did at him. He would not go near her, damned if he would.

How proudly she carried herself, like an Aztec princess. No, Aztec was wrong. He recalled his father mentioning that Caesar Gabaldon was of Yaqui descent. Did the Yaquis have princesses? Not that he cared who her ancestors had been. Maya herself was his real interest.

As if drawn by a force beyond his will, he edged closer. The band was taking a break and a strolling guitarist sang a song he recognized, a song about a white dove flying free while the man left behind must watch the dove from afar no matter how desperately he, too, wished to fly. The words beat within Robert as though they were doves, longing to be free.

He caught a glimpse of his sister, fluttering her fan flirtatiously at a young Chicano but not paying him any real attention. He'd been just Laura's age and equally heart whole when he'd first noticed Maya. He was old enough to be excited by teenage girls—but he hadn't taken any of them seriously. Until Maya.

She'd always been around, he supposed, like most of the workers' kids, but he'd never paid any attention to any of the little girls. Boys didn't play with girls, they played with boys. The happiest times he remembered as a child were those he spent with Sal. Whatever he knew about the ranch and the vineyards he'd learned from Sal.

He might not have noticed Maya when she was a child but at sixteen she'd taken his breath away. Looking at her now, eleven years later, Robert wondered if he'd ever quite gotten his breath back. At sixteen she'd been an unusually pretty girl; at twenty-seven she was a beautiful woman. He couldn't keep away from her now any more than he'd been able to then.

Sal had disappeared. Maya formed part of a circle but Robert couldn't help noticing that she seemed to be in the group without being in it. He pushed through to her.

As though aware he was approaching, she turned, her smoky yellow eyes widening as they focused on him.

"It's nice to see you out of uniform," he said, knowing the words were inane but unable to think of any others.

To his surprise, her face reddened as though he'd said something insulting. "I notice *you're* not in costume." Her voice was tart.

"Siegfried crossed my mind but chain mail didn't seem appropriate. Or armor. Or German opera." God, how patronizing he sounded. Every word he spoke seemed worse than the one before.

"I thought you might come as a Viking."

"Is that how you see me?"

She raised an eyebrow. "As a ruthless invader, you mean? Robbing, pillaging, taking by force?"

He smiled wryly. "I set myself up for that one. But I'm neither a Viking nor Siegfried. I'm merely your average, everyday American male."

Her raised eyebrow told him she didn't accept his description of himself. Robert touched her arm with his fingertips. "What am I, then?"

"A very capable doctor." Her words were cool but he'd felt her momentary quiver under his touch.

"Nothing more?" he asked.

She smiled faintly. "Nothing less, anyway."

A glance showed Robert that either the group had edged away from them, or, without conscious volition, they'd drifted apart from the others. But they were still surrounded by the noisy crowd.

"Have you eaten?" he asked, pitching his voice to be heard over the band.

She shook her head.

Taking her arm, he drew her close to his side, protecting her from jostling as he pushed through the throng until they reached the bank of the creek behind the clinic. Other partygoers sat on the grass with plates of food and cans of soda or beer. Robert strode past them.

"Wait," Maya protested, tugging to free herself. "You're going the wrong way. The food table's in the other direction."

"Too crowded." He held firmly to her arm, urging her along. "We'll eat somewhere else."

"But I came with someone. I can't just—"

"I'll leave a note on Sal's truck. He won't mind."

"What about your sister?"

"I'll tell Sal to give her a ride home."

Not wanting to make a scene, Maya waited until they'd passed all the couples lounging on the grass before she dug in her heels, forcing Robert to a halt.

"All I did was say no when you asked if I'd eaten," she said. "I didn't agree to have dinner with you."

He looked down at her, his eyes unreadable in the darkness. "If I'd brought you a plate of barbecued beef, would you have refused to eat it in my company?"

"No, but—"

"What's wrong with a bit of peace and quiet with our food?"

He was cornering her as he always seemed to do. If she said she didn't want to be alone with him it would sound as though she were afraid. Of him. Of herself. Of what might happen. Maya gritted her teeth. In a sense she was but she refused to admit any such fears to him.

"Viking tactics," she muttered, giving up and continuing on with him.

He didn't reply until they reached his car. "*Paloma blanca,* my longboat awaits," he said, opening the door for her with a flourish.

He rejoined her after sticking a note under the wiper of Sal's pickup, started the car and pulled away from the curb.

"Why did you call me white dove?" she asked.

"There's a song—" He paused, shaking his head. "In the old days," he continued after a moment, "the Vikings took caged doves on their voyages across the Atlantic. Every so often they'd release one. If it flew toward the land they'd left and didn't return, they'd know they hadn't gone far enough. If it circled and came back to the longboat, they were at the point of no return. If it flew ahead of them and didn't return, they rejoiced because they knew they were close to their destination."

Interesting, but how did it apply to what he'd called her? Maya wondered. She was certainly not Robert's guide. Nor was she, no matter what he might think, his prey—as a dove would be to a hawk.

"I see you've boned up on Vikings," she said.

He shrugged. "At one time I thought it was important to know where my genes came from. As behavior clues. Haven't you studied the Yaquis?"

Taken aback, Maya nodded cautiously. She had no idea Robert knew her grandfather's ancestry.

"Still, you, like me, are actually an American." He spoke emphatically, as though trying to prove a point.

She nodded again. "True. At the same time, I can't deny the heritage of my ancestors."

"Is that why they call you *La Curandera?*"

She shot him an exasperated glance. "I'm a nurse. As you well know." Her tone warned him she didn't care to discuss the matter.

"And a damned good nurse. The clinic's fortunate to have you. *I'm* fortunate to have you." He swerved to the left, pulling into the parking lot of a small unpretentious restaurant on the edge of town. "Good, they're not too busy."

The owner greeted Robert by name, seating them at a table in the far corner. Maya, who'd all but forgotten what she was wearing, remembered when she grew conscious of the way Robert looked at her.

"The Poblana peasant women used to wear dresses like this in the old days," she said, resisting the impulse to readjust the low neckline.

"Very colorful—as I'm sure the Poblana men would agree." He leaned forward. "I thought I smelled orange blossoms in the car—you've braided them into your hair."

"I happen to live in the middle of an orange grove."

He touched her hair, his hand lingering while his gaze sought hers. "Charming."

His eyes were such a warm, soft brown, his gaze so frankly admiring that she was almost persuaded it was safe to admit to herself how she enjoyed his touch and how eager she was for more.

Instead, she drew back and deliberately picked up the menu. She'd been fooled by the message in those velvet brown eyes before, she wouldn't be again.

When she declined a before-dinner drink, he settled for wine with the meal. She chose the shepherd's pie, he the beef diablo and he ordered a rosé made by a small winery to the north of Thompsonville.

She tasted the wine, found it pleasant to the tongue and said so. "Sal told me the winery uses Pierson damaged and machine-picked Thompsons for blending," she added.

Maya, who'd picked Pierson grapes from the time she was old enough to be trusted not to bruise them, knew exactly what Sal had meant. The vineyards were largely planted with Thompson seedless, the leading table grape. Unlike wine grapes that would be crushed anyway, table grapes had to be perfect so they were hand-picked.

Robert shrugged. "I don't concern myself with the vineyards."

She raised her eyebrows. "Perhaps you ought to. They're yours, after all."

"Don't you start in. Having to listen to Sal is bad enough."

Ignoring the thread of anger running through his seemingly offhand response, she persisted. "When it concerns the Pierson vineyards, Sal knows what he's talking about. Your—" She paused, thinking twice about mentioning his father. She would never speak of Robert's father to him. *Never.* "Your mother shouldn't be expected to handle everything and Laura's too young."

"Damn the vineyards! I didn't bring you here to discuss Pierson's Pride."

"What did you bring me here to discuss?"

"Us!" He flung the word at her as though it were a glove challenging her to a duel.

"There's nothing to discuss. I was under the impression we worked together very well."

"Who's talking about work?"

"I am. What else is there to talk about?"

"You know damn well. I see it in your eyes, hear it in your voice, feel it when I touch you." He gripped her hand. "Don't try to deny what's between us because if you do I won't believe you."

Maya felt as though his hand had closed around her heart.

Robert saw by her expression that he was moving too fast. When he was near Maya his raw need for her made him forget every bit of finesse he'd learned over the years. She made him feel like the Viking raider she accused him of being, ready to fling the reluctant maiden over his shoulder and sail off with her as his captive.

As he'd more or less tried to do once before. Eleven years before, on a night that didn't bear thinking about. Good God, he was twenty-nine now, not eighteen. The least he could do was act his age. Taking a deep breath, he forced himself to release her hand and lean back in his chair.

"Okay," he said hoarsely, "let's talk about work."

Although it was going to be damned difficult to keep his mind on the clinic when every breath she took revealed the upper swells of her breasts. The way it aroused him you'd think he'd never seen a woman's breasts before.

She smiled faintly. "What if I'd rather discuss grapes?"

Robert relaxed, his tension ebbing. If she could tease him, he hadn't completely blown it. "Grapes? All I know is the Thompson is called the sultana in Australia and the oval kishmish in Asia Minor, where it came from."

"Kishmish? You're making that up."

He put his hand over his heart. "I swear it's true. And, let's see, there's something called the Q10 factor that affects plant respiration."

"I think I prefer human respiration. You seem to know as much about the anatomy of plants as you do people—I'm impressed." Her tone was only half-teasing.

"One of the reasons I went into medicine was because science provides concrete answers. Cause and effect. Remedies."

"Hard science doesn't offer all the answers in medicine," Maya countered. "Or furnish all the cures. I happen to believe very strongly in intangibles such as the laying on of hands."

"The power of suggestion, you mean."

She shook her head. "Not only that. Some people possess a healing energy that they can transfer to a person who's sick."

He frowned. "That's never been proven."

"Those who are able to use it can feel the energy flow. And so can the patient. If it works, isn't that proof enough?"

"Not for me. What's to say it's not simply the power of suggestion? Self-hypnosis?"

Maya's mouth tightened and he thought she meant to launch a rebuttal. Instead, she picked up the salad fork and attacked her greens.

He realized he'd touched a sore point. As he began on his own salad he wondered if it had anything to do with this *curandera* business. She hadn't liked him mentioning that earlier.

Her grandfather had been known locally as a native healer but Robert was under the impression that the old man's reputation as a *curandero* arose from the concoctions of herbs and plants he brewed for his Chicano customers. Maya certainly didn't do anything of that sort. Did she?

As she moved her left arm, light glinted off the bracelet she wore. Looking closely he saw a silver snake, old, judging by the dull finish of the silver, a so-called eternity snake because its mouth gripped its tail. One baleful red eye stared back at him, reflecting the light. He thought it might be a ruby.

"Unusual bracelet," he said.

She laid down her fork to caress the snake's incised scales. "It's Yaqui. I always wear it."

Maya hadn't had the bracelet on that night she bathed naked in the pool. "Always?" he asked before he thought.

Her amber gaze slashed across his face and he knew he'd lost any ground he might have gained. Worse, he'd brought to his own mind the shimmering image of her in the moonlight. He set his teeth against the surge of desire the memory evoked.

"I hope this is hot enough for you, Doctor," a voice said in his ear as the waitress removed his salad and slid his steak *diablo* in front of him.

His gaze inadvertently caught Maya's and he swore he saw a gleam of laughter in her eyes before she looked down at her shepherd's pie.

He wanted her as he'd never wanted another woman but damned if he wasn't beginning to like her, as well. What did she think of him? She'd mentioned he was okay as a doctor but it wasn't Dr. Pierson who wanted to make love to her, it was Robert, the man. He grimaced. She'd made it pretty clear how she felt about that man.

Ruthless. Taking by force. A pillager.

The evening wasn't turning out at all as he'd hoped. As he'd wished. Yet she was here, sitting across from him, eating with him, talking to him. Wasn't it a beginning of sorts?

Did she have the slightest idea how being near her and not being able to touch her tantalized him? During clinic hours the volume of patients left no time to think about anything else, but they weren't at the clinic now.

Later tonight he'd take her home to her house in the orange grove. There, surrounded by the tempting sweetness of blossoms, he'd damn well have to bid her the chastest of good-nights. He wouldn't dare kiss her. One kiss might undermine what control he could manage and he'd turn into exactly what the past had made her fear he was.

When the sports car pulled between the rows of trees into her driveway, Maya struggled to remain calm.

I won't disgrace myself by bolting from the car and rushing to my door before he gets out, she told herself firmly. I won't give him the satisfaction of knowing he's rattled me. If he tries to kiss me, I'll play ice maiden.

Robert stopped the car and came around to open her door. She hoped her exit seemed casual, though she was so tense she doubted it. If he so much as touched her she thought she might fly apart.

"The moon's gibbous," he said. "It'll soon be full."

Damn him! He'd said that on purpose to remind her what had happened during the previous full moon when she'd been foolish enough to trespass on Pierson property. She would *not* react, she'd ignore him.

"Thank you for taking me to dinner." Her words were stiff. She couldn't help it.

"My pleasure." He caught her hand as she started for her door. "It really was, you know."

Why did his touch affect her so acutely? Any ice she might have conjured up was already melting from no more than the warmth of his hand holding hers. She didn't want to feel this way, didn't want his touch. Yet she couldn't bring herself to move. Nor could she think of anything to say.

"If I were your sister I'd resent your leaving me behind," she finally blurted out.

"But you're not my sister."

Didn't he realize every cell in her body was giving her that same message?

"Anyway, Laura and Sal are old friends," he added. "He took my place as her big brother when I left for Stanford."

"That's nice." How inane could she get? Next she'd be telling him to have a nice evening.

"Well, good night," she said, edging toward her door, hoping he'd take the hint and leave.

He kept his hold on her hand, following her. Still, she was getting closer to shutting herself safely inside. When at last she was near enough to use her key, she sighed in relief and tugged her hand free.

A mistake.

He lifted his hand and his fingers trailed lightly down her cheek. "Good night, Maya."

She stared up at him, mesmerized by the caress, afraid and wanting at the same time. His hand dropped. He leaned toward her. She held her breath.

Suddenly he turned abruptly and, with a muttered curse, strode toward his car.

She knew exactly how he felt.

Chapter Five

Maya ushered the last patient, Jaime Gonzalez, from an examining room. The old man had a badly infected foot but had refused hospitalization.

"Remember to soak your foot twice a day," she said in Spanish to make certain he understood. "It's very important."

He answered in heavily accented English. "*Sí*, me, I no forget. I do what you say."

"What the doctor says," she corrected.

Mr. Gonzalez held up the packets of the mild disinfectant she'd given him. "Me, I put in water, like you say."

"That's right. One packet for each soak. And don't forget to take the pills the doctor gave you. Four times a day, remember."

As she escorted the hobbling old man into the waiting room, she saw Robert hunched over the logbook on

Pat's desk. Pat was gone and Angela was getting ready to leave.

Maya didn't know why she'd expected everything to be different after the night Robert had all but kidnapped her for dinner. It wasn't. A week later, far from being eased, the tension between them had increased to the point where it had begun to affect her work. She was so aware of him she had difficulty concentrating on anything else. Something must be done, and soon. But what?

She shut the outside door after Mr. Gonzalez and turned to hurry across the waiting room, wanting to collect her bag and leave before Angela left her alone with Robert.

"You know, Joe has a good billing system going here," Robert said to Angela. His voice was tinged with surprise.

"Joe's a real nut for order," Angela said. "He brought in a bunch of forms and helped Pat and me understand all the ins and outs. Seemed like a lot of extra work at first but it sure pays off when billing time rolls around." She grimaced. "Not that we collect anywhere near half, but our people try to pay what they can. It means a lot to them to know we'll never dun them."

"The way Joe dresses, I didn't figure he'd have this compulsion for order."

Angela laughed. "The poor man needs a wife who'll buy his clothes and lay them out for him." Her eyes flicked over Robert. "Unlike you, Doctor."

Robert grinned at her. "I'm not sure whether to say thanks or not."

"Have you heard how he's getting along?" Angela asked.

"I talked to Joe's doctor this morning. Joe came through the second operation in good shape but it looks like you'll be stuck with me for at least six more weeks, minimum."

Angela shook her head. "He worked himself into the hospital, that's what he did. Never took a vacation. I warned him it was going to kill him and it sure came close. What he needs is a partner, but try to find a doctor who wants to work for peanuts. Everybody's in medicine for the money."

Belatedly, Angela seemed to realize she was talking to a fast-track San Francisco internist and she grew flustered. "I guess it's time I left. Good night, folks."

Maya, who'd lingered at the inner door to listen to the conversation, fled to the lounge, where she recovered her bag and ducked out the back door, once more successfully avoiding being alone with Robert. Tomorrow was Saturday. No clinic hours. No Robert. No tension.

Why did that make her feel let down?

Saturday morning, early, she drove to Sal's place and found him in the field beside his modest cottage leading Padrino toward the horse stall to be saddled.

"I really appreciate you lending me your horse," she said as she walked beside Sal. "I thought maybe you'd decide I wasn't to be trusted after I left the party without telling you last week."

"I didn't mind you going off with Rob," he said. "What I didn't like was being stuck driving Laura home. She's—"

"Helloo!" a woman's voice called. "Sal!"

Maya and Sal turned to look back at the cottage. A yellow convertible was parked behind Maya's VW. Laura stood beside it, waving.

"Speak of the devil," Maya said.

"You don't know how true those words are!" Sal spoke fervently. He didn't explain further because Laura had come through the gate and was running across the field toward them.

"You know Maya Najero, don't you?" Sal asked when she reached them.

Laura's slight frown was replaced by a brilliant smile. "Maya! You're Sal's cousin."

Maya nodded, thinking that, except for her blue eyes and blond hair, Laura resembled her father more than her mother. She was pleasant looking rather than pretty, with an all-embracing smile that made Maya remember George Pierson.

"You remind me of your father," Maya said impulsively.

"Do I really?" Laura seemed pleased but almost immediately she focused her attention on Sal. "I thought maybe we could go riding later today?" she said to him.

"Maya's borrowing Padrino," he said. "Anyway, you know I have to work."

Laura's lower lip drooped. "You always say you have to work. Mr. Fairfax takes Saturdays off. I don't know why you can't."

Sal shrugged. "He's the manager. I'm the foreman." His words were clipped, his tone curt.

Maya wondered why, since Sal was usually friendly. She recalled Robert telling her that Sal was like Laura's big brother. He certainly wasn't behaving that way at the moment. Laura looked positively crushed.

"You talk to him," Laura said to her. "Tell him he works too hard."

Maya thought for a moment before saying lightly, "Sal doesn't work any harder than your brother. Face it—men think the world will fall apart if they aren't on the job, holding things together, while we women know we're really the ones who provide the glue.''

Laura laughed. ''Maybe you and I can go riding sometime if Sal's so determined to work. Okay?''

Maya nodded toward Padrino. ''I'm going now. Want to join me?''

''Oh, gee, I'd like to but I have a tennis lesson this morning. Another time?''

''Fine.'' Maya decided she liked Laura. Robert's sister not only looked like their father but had a similar open and friendly personality.

Why was Sal so cold to the poor girl?

Laura didn't leave immediately, lingering while Sal saddled Padrino, and the truth finally hit Maya. Laura had a crush on Sal.

With a fourteen-year age gap between them plus the other differences, obviously Sal didn't reciprocate. Apparently his brusqueness didn't discourage Laura so it looked as though he'd have to take sterner measures. Any kind of romantic relationship between them was certainly doomed before it began.

Sal knew, and Laura should, the deep chasm between an owner of a Valley vineyard and a Chicano who worked there.

Maya Najero had learned that bitter lesson early. But even if she did bring herself to tell Laura, she had no assurance the girl would believe that what had happened between Maya and Robert in the past applied to Laura and Sal.

In the years before Maya or Robert was born, George Pierson had made the same mistake his daughter teetered on the verge of making, but he was no longer alive to counsel Laura. Even if he was alive, when did a teenage girl who imagined herself in love ever listen to anyone?

It may be impossible to convince Laura, Maya decided, but I sure as hell can tell Sal he'd better find a quick way to end Laura's crush. And I will, as soon as I get him alone.

Obviously Laura meant to hang around until she left, so that time wasn't now. Maya swung onto Padrino, waved to them and rode toward the hills east of town.

Though it was still early morning, the June breeze was warm, promising a hot day, typical weather for Thompsonville at this time of year. By noon the heat of the sun would drive everyone either to seek deep shade or a swimming pool or to escape into an air-conditioned building. The next three months would be much the same. But she didn't miss San Diego's more temperate climate. This was where she'd grown up, this was the way weather was supposed to be.

As a child, instead of a swimming pool she'd had Ría Luna, Moon Creek. Her grandfather never owned an air conditioner but he'd built his cabin under several large valley oaks for shade. Her mother, like herself, had grown up in that cabin. It was gone now, swept away when the creek overflowed its banks in a flood year. The land the cabin had stood on belonged to the Piersons.

"My father gave Caesar Gabaldon permission to build that cabin," George Pierson had told her once. "Your grandfather had a natural affinity for grapes—he was never wrong about the best time for pruning and the right time for picking. I valued him as much as my father did."

But George had never spoken of her mother. It had been old Caesar who'd told her the poignant story after that terrible night with Robert.

"Your mother, she was a beautiful woman, as you are," her grandfather had said. "Sometimes beauty is a curse, my child. As a young man George Pierson was drawn to my Estella as the sphinx moth is drawn to a grapevine in flower. And she gave her love to him as freely as the flower gives its nectar to the moth. Just as the moth causes the vine to wither and die, so did her love for him eventually destroy your mother."

Her grandfather's words had jolted Maya from her black despair. "But my mother married another man. She married my father!"

"Perhaps it was fortunate your father didn't live long enough to understand Estella's heart was not his," Caesar said. "He gave your mother the child she longed for, but even your birth and her love for you were not enough to save Estella. Unlike your mother, you are strong, Maya. You will survive."

I *am* strong, she told herself as Padrino trotted along a dirt trail leading into the hills. And smart enough not to repeat past mistakes.

Robert flung a saddle on Emperor, a black stallion as dark as the grape he was named for—if not as sweet in disposition. He didn't mind; he relished the challenge of handling a fractious horse.

As he rode away from the stable, he approached Sal, who was parking his pickup, and reined in.

"Don't you ever take a day off?" he said. "It's Saturday, you know."

Sal eyed him levelly. "I know, you know, but do the grapes know?"

Robert shrugged. "Laura told me Maya borrowed Padrino. Any idea where she's riding?"

Sal shook his head, unsmiling. "I think she wanted to be alone."

Robert waved and rode off, aware of Sal's disapproving stare, making Sal the second person he'd annoyed this morning. His mother had been the first.

"All I want to do is give a simple little party," she'd insisted as she poured herself a second cup of coffee. "The least you can do is be agreeable."

"I don't call a guest list of thirty-five little," he countered. "Nor hiring a combo for dancing simple. If you want to invite your friends and Laura's, fine. But don't start trotting out local eligible maidens for my inspection. I have no intention of getting married in the foreseeable future."

"The things you accuse me of!"

"Because I know exactly how your mind works."

Susan Pierson widened her blue eyes, so like Laura's. "That's not fair, Robbie. I planned this get-together solely to give you a chance to socialize with your old friends."

He sighed with exasperation. His mother was a past master at laying on guilt trips. He was stuck with the party so he might as well be gracious. As he was about to capitulate, an idea slid into his mind. If he had to socialize, he ought to enjoy it.

"If the party's for me, I have the right to invite someone."

Susan blinked but quickly recovered. "Naturally. I'll add your friend to the guest list if you'll give me the name."

"She's a nurse I work with at the clinic. Maya Najero."

Susan's mouth tightened. "If this is a joke, I don't appreciate its humor."

"I'm not joking."

"You want to invite that woman's daughter into my house?"

"Our house. Anyway, that's all in the past. Estella's dead."

"Like mother, like daughter," Susan muttered, scowling at him.

He scowled back, sorry he'd brought Maya's name into this but damned if he'd back down as he usually did when his mother applied the pressure. He was no longer her little boy.

Susan took a deep breath and did her best to look reasonable. "Even if I did invite her—do think, Robbie, how out of place she'd feel. After all, there won't be another Chicano at the party."

Robert tried to control his anger. It would be of no use to lecture his mother on prejudice, no use to point out how behind the times her attitude was. After all, she reflected the feeling of most of Thompsonville—there were growers and there were pickers and never the twain shall meet socially.

"Please add Maya Najero to your guest list." His voice held a chill.

"Since you insist." His mother's tone had been even chillier.

Riding toward the eastern hills on Emperor, he had the feeling Maya's attitude would be frostier yet when she discovered what he'd done.

It wasn't wise to disturb ghosts from the past. So why had he? He knew the answer. Because meeting Maya again had roused them anyway and there'd be no rest for him until the past was exorcised. If that was possible.

His mood lightened as the spirit of the hunt began to sing in his blood. She was somewhere in these hills, he was positive, and he meant to find her. To hell with Sal's warning and his mother's prejudice. And with Maya's own campaign to avoid him except when they saw patients at the clinic.

He had a hunch he knew where she'd ridden so he dug his heels in, urging Emperor into a lope.

Leaning against a pine trunk in a small grove a mile north of where Caesar Gabaldon's cabin had been, Maya heard a horse's hoofbeats and the creak of a saddle. She tensed before the rider crested the hill. She didn't have to see him to know who he was. Conquering her impulse to mount Padrino and gallop off, she stood her ground under the shade of the pines. Why should she run from Robert Pierson? She could handle him and she would.

She watched him ride down the incline toward her, telling herself her increasingly rapid pulse was due to the rush of adrenaline any confrontation provokes. The fact he was who he was had nothing to do with it.

He reined in, dismounted, tethered his black stallion near Padrino and stood looking at her.

"I thought you'd be here," he said.

"I came this way to see if anything was left of my grandfather's cabin. I found nothing except memories."

"His cabin wasn't here. This is where we met."

She nodded.

"I've never forgotten the day we met." His voice was low, hoarse.

Maya found it difficult to take a breath. "I remember." She could scarcely push the words from her dry throat.

It had been a late afternoon in July. He'd been riding a beautiful palomino but once she saw him she hardly noticed the horse. She knew immediately the handsome blond young man was Robert Pierson; she'd watched him from afar many times.

She could tell he didn't recognize her. Why should he? He didn't live at home most of the year or go to the local schools. He attended a boarding school in the Bay area.

Mesmerized, she watched him halt the palomino less than a foot from where she sat on a blanket reading. He slid off the horse and eased down beside her.

"May I join you?" he asked.

"You already have." How cool and collected she sounded, even though her heart hammered against her ribs. Robert Pierson was actually sitting beside her!

"What are you reading?" Without waiting for an answer, he lifted the book from her hands, his fingers brushing against hers for a brief second.

Maya swallowed, incapable of speech as she tried to cope with the quivery feeling in her stomach caused by his touch.

"The Lady of the Lake," he read and glanced at her, smiling. "I'm hopeless when it comes to poetry." He opened the book to the first page. "I thought maybe I'd find your name written here but, if it was, the page has been torn out."

The book had been her mother's. The page had been missing the first time Maya ever opened the book.

She smiled at him, at a loss for words.

"You're not taking the hint," he said. "I really would like to know your name."

His eyes were the velvety brown of the cattails that grew in the low spots along the creek. She'd been trans-fixed by the way those brown eyes looked at her.

And, damn it, he was looking at her the same way now. Worse, she was as mesmerized as she'd been at sixteen.

"You wouldn't tell me your name," Robert said. "You wouldn't tell me where you lived. The bicycle propped against the tree fooled me—I thought you must have ridden from town along one of the fire trails. I never once thought of old Caesar's cabin." He took a step toward her and reached for her hands.

She stepped back. "No. Don't."

He stopped. "You were the prettiest girl I'd ever seen. You still are."

"I should never have agreed to meet you again," she said, remembering against her will. "Somehow it seemed as if I couldn't say no. The first time we met was on a hot afternoon but I always thought of what happened to me as being moonstruck."

He half smiled. "It didn't happen only to you. We were both moonstruck. I couldn't stay away from you. Not knowing your name made it even more exciting. I think a part of me really didn't want to discover who you were because it kept what was between us mysterious and unreal, apart from ordinary life."

Magic had been her word for those secret and won-derful twilight meetings here in the pine grove when they'd exchanged kisses and caresses until she was light-headed with what she believed was love.

The last time they met had not been here but under the sycamores where Ría Luna formed a pool among the boulders. The moon had risen, round and perfect, scat-tering silver light through the branches, touching the pool with its unearthly glimmer, creating an enchanted oasis.

The moon had also been full this May when she'd unwisely returned there, never dreaming he was anywhere near Thompsonville. She should have confronted him about it immediately but she hadn't had the nerve. Until now.

"You spied on me!" she accused.

Robert blinked, frowning.

"In May," she added. "I know it was you sneaking through the sycamores."

"If you mean at the pool," he said, "I wasn't sneaking or spying. I was merely taking an evening stroll on Pierson property."

She glared at him. "You never change, do you? I might have known you'd blame me for trespassing rather than admit you were wrong."

"I wasn't accusing you, I was just—"

Gripped by a fury that had its roots in the past, she scarcely heard his words. "You blamed me then, you blame me now. Nothing is ever your fault, is it? Piersons can do no wrong, Piersons are perfect. Never mind what you accused me of, I'll never forgive you for what you said about my mother. Or how you ruined—" She broke off, choked by the lump in her throat that heralded tears.

She refused to cry in front of Robert. Turning on her heel, she started for Padrino, intending to ride off.

He grasped her arm, jerking her to a halt. "Just one damn minute. We're going to thrash this out here and now. If you think I—" His beeper went off, the electronic blips startling both of them.

He muttered a curse, unhooked it from his belt and flicked a switch. "Dr. Pierson."

Over the static, a voice spoke faintly, many of the words unintelligible. "Emergency...convulsion... eight months...hospital..."

He dropped her arm and returned the beeper to his belt. "Don't think this is over and done with," he warned, striding to his horse.

As Robert urged Emperor into a lope, he tried to speculate what he'd find waiting for him at the hospital but found he couldn't easily block the past from his mind. He was every bit as guilty as Maya had insisted— the whole damn mess had been his fault. Not because he thought Piersons were perfect, but because he'd been eighteen and in love for the first time in his life.

He smiled ruefully. Two mistakes he'd never make again—being eighteen and falling in love.

Ten years ago Maya had been more beautiful than the moonlight, more mysterious than the night, a dream he hadn't known existed until they met. He hadn't exactly been the sophisticated man of the world he liked to pretend he was but he hadn't been totally naive, either. He knew she was an innocent and it thrilled him to realize he was the first man to stir her passion.

He'd never meant to hurt her. Being unkind to her was the farthest thing from his mind. Until the afternoon he passed the café in Visalia and saw her seated at a table inside—with his father, who was laughing at something she'd said. The shock of seeing them together paralyzed him until it filtered through to him who she must be.

His mystery girl was Maya Gabaldon Najero. She and his father were obviously friends.

How unhappy and hurt his mother would be if she knew George Pierson was having lunch with Estella Gabaldon's daughter.

Robert couldn't recall a time in his life when his mother hadn't complained about his father neglecting her.

"He doesn't care about me," she'd often say. "He never wanted to marry me. He wanted *her*." Later, his mother began bemoaning the fact that George Pierson was taking an interest in Estella's daughter. "He wants to finance her education—if you can imagine! Wasting money better spent on you or on poor little Laura."

Robert had never felt his father cared about him. He couldn't remember when his father last took *him* to lunch. Or laughed at something he'd said. Estella's daughter was more important to him than his own son.

Damn it, Maya was his! She had no business being there with his father.

Robert had brooded for the rest of the day about how he'd been betrayed by both his father and Maya. By that evening all his unhappiness was shunted into anger at Maya. To think he'd been wondering how to tell her that he loved her— What a fool he was!

He wouldn't show up at the sycamore grove that night; he wouldn't ever see her again. But when the evening darkened, he couldn't stay away. His anger somehow intensified his desire to be with her. The anticipation of holding her in his arms drew him from the house, across the fields and into the grove.

When he saw her silvered by moonlight, her beauty caught at his heart. As he pulled her close, for a moment he forgot everything but his need for her. At first she responded eagerly to his kisses and caresses, fueling his arousal. She was warm and soft, smelling of honeysuckle and her own exciting woman scent. She tasted as sweet as a ripe grape, fresh picked from the vine. She was enchantment, she was love.

He meant to have all of her, make her completely his. No one else would have her. Ever.

She murmured a protest when he bore her to the ground and she tried to draw away. But she didn't begin to really struggle until he started to pull off her shorts.

"No, please, don't," she begged.

He couldn't stop, wouldn't stop. He was wild with need.

She started to cry, gasping, frightened sobs that pierced his haze of desire.

God! He was on the verge of raping her! Robert flung himself away, shocked and frightened by what he'd almost done. He wasn't that kind of a man. Never!

Guilt stricken, despising himself and throbbing with unfulfilled need, Robert awkwardly put his clothes in order. Her muffled sobs set his teeth on edge.

Damn it, he'd stopped, hadn't he? Anger filled the emptiness in him. He turned on her.

"I'll bet you don't say no to my father." His voice was hoarse, almost a growl. "Your mother didn't, did she? She was his mistress. And you—"

"Shut up!" she screamed. "I hate you, hate you, hate you." She flew at him, pummeling him with her fists.

When he fended her off, she glared at him. "I'll hate you as long as we both live, Robert Pierson. I hope to God I never see you again."

And then she was gone, running through the trees, her dark hair streaming behind her.

Shamed and heartsick at what he'd done, what he'd accused her of, silently he echoed her fervent plea. God grant that he never met Maya Najero again.

Chapter Six

Maya drove to the clinic on Monday, her mind a whirlpool of emotions caused by the Saturday confrontation with Robert. In a matter of minutes she'd have to face him again. Luckily it would be at the clinic—their only neutral ground up until now. She must make certain it remained neutral.

She couldn't permit the past to override the present; she refused to allow her feelings to interfere with her work.

Robert, unshaven, was already in his office when she walked down the corridor. She paused. Though he had an electric razor in his hand, he was making no effort to begin shaving.

"You look as though you spent all night at the hospital," she said.

He nodded. "Most of the day, too. First we had to section a convulsing mother eight months along—to save the baby—then I admitted three very sick kids with encephalitis.'' He ran a hand over his stubbled jaw. ''I wanted to take the baby on Saturday but do you think I could find one OB man or general surgeon to do the surgery? Damn these local doctors!''

Maya knew that Robert, with his specialty in internal medicine, wouldn't do a cesarean section. Even if he wanted to, his hospital privileges didn't include surgery.

''How did you finally persuade one of them to operate?'' she asked.

''I cornered Ken Townsend when he finished delivering one of his patients early Sunday morning. I told him the hell with his policy of not taking Medi-Cal cases, if he refused to help my patient he'd be guilty of infanticide. The mother was already brain-dead, no way could I ship her to the County Hospital in Bakersfield in time—we had to take that baby before Mama's heart stopped. He was mad as hell at me but he cooled down some when we extracted a squalling five-pound boy. The mother died an hour later.''

''What from?''

''I suspect Western equine encephalitis in her case as well as the other three but the lab reports aren't back yet.''

Remembering his beeper call on Saturday, Maya asked, ''Was she the emergency having convulsions?''

He nodded yes. ''I couldn't save her but at least her baby's doing well, thanks to Townsend's guilty conscience. I just may have made a convert there. Or at least set him to reordering his priorities. You'd think it was going to kill the doctors around here to do a little *pro bono* work.''

She didn't bother to remind him the local doctors hadn't changed since she was a child. Then, as now, poor people seemed to be beneath their notice.

"I'm glad you were able to save the baby," she said. "I hope we don't get a run on encephalitis cases."

"I'm afraid we will. The wet spring bred hordes of mosquitoes. My hunch is we'll be seeing more cases in the clinic this week. I plan to call the mosquito control district people today and alert them to a possible epidemic. I might phone the local vets, too, and find out if they're seeing a lot of sick horses. A rise in human cases usually follows an epidemic among horses."

Maya knew there was no drug effective against the arbovirus causing the disease—the patient had to fight off the bug on his own. Adults usually had only mild symptoms but children under a year often were severely ill and some died. No matter how long she worked as a nurse, she would never easily accept the death of a child. She fervently hoped there'd be no more deaths if they did have an epidemic on their hands.

"Please tell me this will be a light day," Robert said, yawning.

"We haven't had a light day since I started working here." Hardening her heart against his obvious fatigue, she added, "You'd better turn on that razor."

"I don't suppose I could talk you into shaving me while I catch a short nap."

Maya raised her eyebrows. "You're the doctor, not the patient. All you get from me is a cup of coffee."

"I think I'm past the point where caffeine can help—but it can't hurt. Thanks."

She went to fetch the coffee, relieved they'd kept the conversation away from the personal. She wondered if he had the same feeling she did—that they were treading on a fragile bridge of civility over an abyss of roiling emotions. One wrong word could send them plunging into danger.

Thank heaven clinic Mondays were always hectic.

The day passed in a blur of sick children and worried parents. Robert's prediction of a possible encephalitis epidemic seemed to be coming true. Injuries and chronically ill adults added to the patient load, so it was after six before the waiting room was empty.

Though Angela, like Maya, didn't get paid extra for working overtime, she stayed on as usual until the last patient left.

"It's no trouble," she confided to Maya as she got ready to leave. "My husband, old macho himself, learned the hard way to start dinner or starve. Surprise! He discovered he liked to cook. Makes a mean *menudo*."

Maya, on her way to the back exit, saw Robert in his office talking on the phone. He gestured when she passed, covering the mouthpiece with his hand. She stopped, waiting.

"I forgot to tell you something," he said. "You'll be getting an invitation from my mother next week. I hope you'll come to the party."

She stared at him. He smiled at her and resumed his phone conversation—with the hospital from the sound of it.

Maya walked slowly to the back door, trying to come to terms with what he'd told her. His mother was inviting Maya Najero to a party at Pierson's Pride? No way. This had to be Robert's idea and somehow he'd gotten his mother to agree.

She was damned if she'd go.

As she pulled from the parking lot, Maya changed her mind. If she didn't show up, Susan Pierson would think she was afraid to come. That wasn't true. She didn't fear any of the Piersons. She'd attend the party—with bells on.

Bells and what else? She couldn't think of one single thing in her closet suitable to wear. Simple yet elegant was the effect she wanted. Unfortunately that combination usually cost a fortune and she was short of money at the moment.

She stopped for take-out green *chile rellenos* from a Mexican café, and by the time she finished eating them at home, she'd decided on the color of the dress. Whatever she came up with would have to be white. As she got ready for bed, she remembered the box of her mother's belongings that Sal had stored for her while she was in San Diego. He'd brought the box to her a week ago but she hadn't yet sorted through it.

How she'd love to wear a dress of her mother's to Susan Pierson's house.

Maya hauled the wooden box from the back of her bedroom closet and cut the sealing tape. The first thing she saw when she pried up the nailed-down cover was a framed wedding picture of her mother and father, one she didn't remember.

She knew from her grandfather that her mother had married in Mexico and lived there until Maya's father was killed in an accident. Then she'd returned to California and Caesar Gabaldon to have her baby. Though her smile in the picture held a hint of sadness, Estella had been a beautiful bride. The groom, Jaime Najero, faced the camera with a jaunty, devil-may-care grin, making Maya sorry she'd never known him.

She had no real memory of her mother, either, and tears came to her eyes as she gazed at the young bride and groom, the strangers who'd been her parents. If they'd lived, would they have had a happy life together? It was a question that had no answer.

Setting the picture carefully on her dresser, she delved back into the box. She found two books, both leather-bound with gold edges, reminding her of *The Lady of the Lake*. These were also poems. Browning. Yeats. Maya opened them and found the first pages missing. Torn out.

She drew in her breath as the reason for the missing pages occurred to her. The books of poetry had been given to her mother by George Pierson and he'd written a message to Estella on the first page. Words of love? She'd never know. Her mother had destroyed what he'd written but kept the books.

"Piersons don't marry Gabaldons," Maya's grand-father had told her. "Young George was not allowed to ask for my Estella's hand. His parents insisted he marry a woman of his own kind. He spoke of running off with Estella, but much as she loved him, she would not go. The truth is he didn't try as hard as he might have to convince her. He was not a fighter. When his engagement to another was announced, I sent Estella to my brother in Mexico, hoping her heart would mend. She met your father and she married him but her heart—" Caesar sighed. "Some broken hearts never heal."

And so Estella had destroyed the messages of love but couldn't bring herself to part with the books. Maya bit her lip as she laid them aside with a fresh understanding of why George Pierson had been so kind to Estella's daughter.

Maya had always longed to be a healer and George had listened to her and given her the chance to become a nurse. It had been, she realized, an atonement for the misery he'd caused her mother. He hadn't been happy himself, if the gossip about the Piersons' troubled marriage could be believed.

More than two lives had been blighted by prejudice.

Her enthusiasm had ebbed by the time she lifted out the clothing at the bottom of the box. But when she saw one of the dresses was a yellowed white, she held it up, recognizing the dress for what it was—a wedding gown. Not the one her mother wore in the picture. This type of dress was what brides in a certain Mexican province married in—or used to. Today tourists bought them.

But this one differed from the commercially made dresses she'd seen. The cotton was soft and fine, the embroidery, white on white, exquisite, the lace handmade. The high waist came just under the breasts, the square-cut neck was low without being immodest. The skirt was ankle-length, generously cut and tiered with lace. She didn't believe the garment had ever been worn.

Maya wondered why her mother had saved this dress but not the gown she'd been married in. Had the Mexican dress been bought for another wedding, one that never took place? A lump rose in her throat. She fought tears. No, she wouldn't cry over the sad wrongs of the past.

The white of the gown had yellowed with age but if she used great care she might be able to restore the original brightness without ruining the fabric.

Maya nodded grimly and found a hanger for the dress. She'd found just the thing to wear to Pierson's Pride.

* * *

Robert fell into bed the minute he walked in the door. His mother woke him at nine, asking if he wanted to eat. About to say no, he realized he was hungry.

She'd had the cook set aside a serving for him and when he wandered into the kitchen his mother placed the dish in the microwave and reheated the shrimp and rice, serving him at the kitchen table.

She sat opposite him, sipping a cup of tea.

"You shouldn't be working such long hours, dear," she said. "Surely you can find some other doctor to take some of the calls for you."

He snorted. "Not in this town. No local doctor will have anything to do with clinic patients. Their attitude makes me mad as hell."

"Well, Robbie, you really can't blame them. These La Raza Clínica people came into Thompsonville and, without consulting a single one of the local physicians, set up in that old building. I'm not so provincial as to mistrust outsiders but I do understand how the Thompsonville doctors must have felt. Surely it would have been common courtesy to try to involve the medical community beforehand."

Robert shook his head. "I doubt that the local docs would have been enthusiastic about seeing La Raza Clínica patients under any circumstances."

"How do you know?"

"Money's their bottom line. It doesn't pay to take care of poor people, even those with Medi-Cal coverage. So they don't. Won't. Yesterday I had to shame Ken Townsend into helping me with a patient."

Susan set down her teacup. "Is that so? Alicia Townsend is on the garden club board with me. She's a lovely person. Very civic-minded."

Robert sighed inwardly. His mother didn't understand; she never would.

After a short silence, Susan said, "I think you should speak to your sister, Robbie."

He blinked. "To Laura? What about?"

"I believe she's been lying to me about where she goes and what she does. It's terribly worrisome. She's eighteen, but not a mature eighteen, and I'm afraid she may be getting in with the wrong crowd. Would you—"

"I'll keep an eye on her and do what I can. Laura and I really don't know each other very well—my fault, I guess—but she doesn't strike me as a liar."

Susan put her hand on his arm. "I'm so glad you came home."

He shifted his shoulders uncomfortably. He hadn't come home, not really. He was staying at the house as a convenience for the time he'd be in Thompsonville.

"It's only temporary," he reminded her, putting his hand over hers for a moment.

She frowned. "That's as may be, but it's really not good for your health to be up all night and still work the next day."

He smiled. His mother never seemed to realize he'd grown up.

The phone rang and he rose to answer it. When he finished speaking to the hospital, he walked onto the side screened porch and stood looking into the night. I'll talk to Sal, he thought. He's likely to know what's going on around town. If he can't tell me what Laura's up to maybe he can find out.

A fleeting scent of orange blossoms borne on the night wind wiped his sister from his mind. What was Maya doing in her orange grove tonight? He had yet to see the inside of her apartment. She couldn't keep him at arm's length forever, past or no past.

He didn't have a chance to talk to Sal until just before noon on Saturday. Fairfax was nowhere around—the manager didn't work on Saturdays—but one of the workers said he thought Sal might be at the irrigation shed.

As Robert walked between the staked grapevines, he caught himself automatically glancing from side to side at the fruiting canes as Sal had taught him, checking the leaves for insect infestation or diseases such as leaf roll. The sun beat down, reminding him why the San Joaquin Valley produced the best table and raisin grapes— all the warm days and nights between April 1 and October 31. Hot days from June through August. It was already in the upper nineties today; Sal would be turning the sprinklers on soon—on for three minutes, off for fifteen, until the thermometer dropped into the eighties—to prevent the leaves from scorching.

Funny how much he remembered about the damn vineyard. The details somehow stuck in his mind. It was hard to get rid of the past.

As he walked up behind the irrigation shed, he heard his sister's voice coming from the other side.

"You used to let me help," she was saying. "I like to help you, Sal. Why is it you never have any time to spend with me anymore?"

Robert frowned, hearing the plea in Laura's voice with dismay. Why was it so important to her to be with Sal?

"You got better things to do than trail after me," Sal muttered.

"Not really. Not things that I want to do." Laura's voice was plaintive. "Don't you like me anymore?"

"Of course I like you." Sal sounded exasperated.

"Then prove it and come riding with me tomorrow."

Robert eased around the corner of the shed. Laura, both her hands on Sal's arm, was staring up at him with a bemused expression. Sal looked uneasy as well as unhappy.

"Look, Laura, I—" He stopped abruptly when he saw Robert. "Your brother's here," he said.

Laura snatched her hands away and crossed her arms over her chest, scowling at Robert. Sal, he thought, seemed both embarrassed and relieved by his appearance.

Robert ambled over to his sister and draped an arm around her shoulders. "How about a friendly game of tennis?" he asked. "Loser buys lunch."

His mother wouldn't be at all pleased to be told her daughter yearned after Sal Ramirez. Not that he planned to tell her. Sal didn't reciprocate Laura's interest, and since his sister would be going to Stanford in the fall, he saw no real problem.

"I'm helping Sal with the sprinklers," she said.

"I don't need help," Sal said firmly. "Go play tennis with Rob."

Laura pouted. After a moment she said, "It isn't fair the way Mr. Fairfax takes every weekend off and expects Sal to do everything. Poor Sal never gets any time off."

Robert raised his eyebrows questioningly at Sal, who shrugged, making Robert decide he'd better have a few words with the new manager. He didn't like being drawn into vineyard business but fair was fair.

"See you later," he told Sal as he led Laura away from the shed.

"Even if he didn't graduate from UC Davis, Sal knows more about grapes than Mr. Fairfax. He's really, really wonderful, don't you think?"

"Mr. Fairfax?" Robert asked, being deliberately obtuse.

Laura poked him in the ribs with her elbow and then pulled away. "Mr. F's a creep. You know I meant Sal. He worries about the vineyard like it was his." She sighed. "I wish I was older."

"That's one thing I can promise you will be."

"When you're eighteen no one takes you seriously. I mean they act like you don't have true feelings and all." Laura glanced sideways at him. "You think I'll get over Sal, don't you?"

Taken aback by her acuteness, Robert tried to frame an answer she'd accept. "Not exactly. I believed I was in love when I was eighteen so I know how painful the feeling can be. Still, I survived."

"And are you completely and irrevocably over her?" Laura demanded.

Robert chose his words with care. "I'll admit I never forgot her, but I realize now it wasn't love."

She looked at him dubiously. "What if you met her again?"

I have, he thought, and it's hell.

Unwilling to go on in that dangerous direction, he changed the focus. "Sal's past thirty. He's a lot older than you."

"What difference does that make? I'm old *enough*." She stopped and faced him, her chin thrust out belligerently. "Is it because he's Chicano?"

"Sal's my friend, Laura."

She stared at him, absently scratching a mosquito bite on her arm. "I wish you lived here all the time, Rob. Mom's impossible to talk to."

"I'm here now. Shall we play tennis?"

Laura shook her head. "Actually I don't feel like tennis. It's too hot."

He was about to suggest a dip in the pool when his beeper went off. The hospital needed him, stat, in a hurry.

By the time he returned home three hours later, Laura had gone somewhere in her yellow convertible. His mother didn't know where. The sprinklers in the vineyard were going automatically, but Sal was nowhere around. Neither was Sal's pickup.

Sal and Laura can't be together, he told himself. Old straight-arrow Sal would never agree to a rendezvous with her. More than likely Laura was off with her friends.

The phone rang. A few moments later, Elsie, their maid, came onto the screened porch. "Miss Najero's on the phone, Doctor."

He nodded, his heart leaping, and strode into the house to use the phone in the library.

"Maya?"

"Laura's at my place," Maya said without preamble. "I don't like the way she looks. She claims she's okay but I won't let her drive home by herself. I'm afraid—" She paused and lowered her voice. "You'd better come over and see for yourself."

Alarm tensed him. Maya wouldn't have called him unless she thought something was radically wrong with his sister.

"I'm on my way."

He ran to his car.

"It's just a bad headache," Laura protested as Maya urged her to stretch out on the couch. "I don't need to lie down."

"You've heard what tyrants nurses are," Maya said with a lightness she didn't feel. "Humor me."

Laura's headache, combined with the fine tremor of her hands, her elevated temperature and the red welts on her arms added up to a conclusion Maya didn't want to reach.

"I guess I really don't feel too good," Laura admitted, closing her eyes with a sigh. "I'm sorry to bother you like this."

"I don't mind."

"Rob'll be provoked. He already sort of yelled at me about Sal and now he has to come rescue me."

"Yelled at you?" Maya echoed indignantly.

"Not really yelled, you know? Kind of a lecture about how he fell in love when he was my age so he knew how I felt and all that but I'd get over it." She opened her eyes, winced and closed them again. "I won't, you know. And I don't think Rob ever got over his love, either. Whoever she was."

Maya stared at her, struck dumb. Robert had been eighteen that fateful summer. When he spoke of being in love, surely he hadn't meant feeling that way about Maya Najero. Never.

He couldn't have loved me and treated me the way he did, Maya told herself. Frightened me. Said those cruel words. If he'd loved me, he wouldn't have deliberately ruined what was between us.

"Don't tell Rob I came here looking for Sal, please?" Laura begged.

Maya had to clear her throat before she could speak. "I won't."

"My head hurts really awful. Couldn't you give me an aspirin or something?"

"We'll wait until your brother examines you, okay?"

"Examines me!" Laura tried to sit up, moaned and fell back. "I'm so dizzy." She began to cry.

Maya knelt beside the couch and held Laura's hand. At the moment she couldn't offer anything more than the reassurance of human touch. She hoped that her tentative diagnosis would prove wrong but she didn't believe it would.

An hour later, Maya, still in shorts and crop top, restlessly turned the pages of an outdated magazine in the lobby of I.R. Thompson Memorial Hospital. As she'd suspected, Laura had been admitted with encephalitis. Maya had ridden in with Robert to help with Laura and he'd asked her to wait for him.

She'd exhausted all possible reading material by the time he strode toward her. Maya rose to meet him. "How is she?"

Robert shook his head. "Semicomatose."

Maya bit her lip. A bad sign. "Why not let me be Laura's private-duty nurse over the weekend?" she asked. Glancing down at her clothes, she added, "I do need to change first."

"I'll drive you home. We've found a nurse who'll stay until eleven but none for the night shift. I really appreciate your offer."

As he spun the Italian coupe from the hospital parking lot, Robert said, "Don't worry about Laura's convertible—I'll send someone to pick it up. I hope—" He broke off, sighing. "She's so young."

Maya knew what he feared to put into words, his hope that Laura would live to drive her car again.

She took a deep breath. Though her acquaintance with Robert's sister was brief, the girl had touched a chord in her, perhaps because of her resemblance to George Pierson.

"I'll do everything I can for Laura," she said.

Without looking at her, Robert reached for Maya's hand and clasped it in his own. She didn't object, aware he needed what she'd offered Laura earlier—the comfort of human touch.

He dropped her off in the drive and spun away in a flurry of dust, hurrying, she knew, back to the hospital. She stood for a time looking after him before turning to walk to the house. Robert must realize, as she did, that medical science's many wonderful discoveries, including the miracle drugs, were useless against the arbovirus that had invaded Laura's body.

She'd promised to do everything she could to save his sister. This meant using all her knowledge, not merely what she'd learned in her nursing courses. She had until eleven o'clock tonight to prepare.

Some called it superstition. Maya believed it was ancient wisdom. Her grandfather had done more than offer herbal potions and he'd passed on his knowledge to her.

"You have the gift, child, as your mother did not," he'd told her. "This gift is never to be taken lightly and should never be refused by the one so honored. At the same time, it must be used sparingly. You must never ask unless the need is great."

When the long blue evening shadows coalesced into true darkness, Maya, wearing nothing but a loose, knee-length, sleeveless cotton shift and thongs, eased from the house and slipped through the orange trees, climbing to the hill in back of the grove. There, she slid off the thongs and stood barefoot in the heat-dried grass, her toes wriggling into the hard-baked dirt below the grass.

She removed the snake bracelet, placed it carefully on the ground in front of her and raised her arms. The moon was not yet up, but since it was waning rather than waxing, the moon would be of little value.

As the ancient Yaqui words her grandfather had taught her came to her tongue, she closed her eyes, concentrating with her entire being as she asked in the old language for the earth, the mother of all, to lend her energy, energy to be borrowed only for healing, energy to be funneled through her for the good of another.

After a time a great serenity settled over her like a blessing and she realized the earth had answered her plea. Though she didn't understand exactly how she knew, it didn't matter.

She was ready.

Chapter Seven

When Maya approached Laura's room, she saw a tall blond older woman talking with Robert in the hall and knew it must be Susan Pierson. She hesitated, then went on.

Robert caught sight of her when she'd almost reached them. He smiled at her, a tired, unhappy smile.

"This is Maya Najero," he said to Susan. "She'll be staying with Laura tonight. Maya, this is my mother."

Maya couldn't manage a smile for Susan Pierson but she murmured a polite greeting.

"How do you do." Susan's words were edged with frost.

"Maya's giving up her free time to be with Laura," Robert said.

"So you told me." Susan's gaze assessed Maya and found her lacking.

She obviously doesn't want me here under any circumstances, Maya thought. But I'm going to help Laura despite her.

"Please excuse me." Stepping past them, she walked into Laura's room.

The girl lay on her right side, an intravenous line feeding into her left arm. The electronic heart monitor showed rapid blips on its screen.

Wilma Larch, the evening charge nurse, greeted her pleasantly. "I understand from Dr. Pierson that you saw the patient earlier," she said. "There hasn't been much change during my shift. Her temperature is still elevated and Laura isn't responding except to painful stimuli."

Which meant Laura was in a coma and didn't react in any way unless she was pricked with a pin or someone pressed on her closed eyelid. Maya didn't plan to try either method. Why inflict pain?

She listened to Wilma explain what had been done for the patient. "Mrs. Pierson wants to stay all night with her daughter," the evening nurse finished.

Maya tensed. If Susan was in the room there'd be no chance for her to carry out her plan. She must be alone with Laura.

"The doctor's trying to talk her out of it," Wilma added, "but Mrs. Pierson is one determined lady." She rolled her eyes. "My mother can be a pain sometimes but that one—" Wilma nodded toward the closed door "—could give lessons to a steamroller."

Maya stepped to the bedside, picked up Laura's limp hand and held it between both of hers. I'm here, she said silently, and one way or another I'll help you.

"Good night then," Wilma said. "And good luck."

"Thank you."

Robert stuck his head in after Wilma left. "I'm driving my mother home," he said. "I'll be back."

Maya, happy and relieved to hear he'd prevailed over Susan, hoped he wouldn't rush to return. She needed time alone with Laura. He wouldn't understand what she was doing and might try to interfere. She couldn't allow any doubt to creep in, lest it interfere with her ability to transfer healing energy.

Letting down the bed rail, she eased Laura onto her back, shifting her so Laura lay at a slight angle, her head close to Maya. After sliding off the silver bracelet, Maya placed it on Laura's forehead and put her left hand on top of the bracelet, then crossed her right hand over her left.

This was much like the laying on of hands advocated by some holistic believers—except for the bracelet. Maya used the bracelet because her grandfather had taught her that silver conducted healing energy better than any other metal. And the snake shape of her silver bracelet symbolized the dream healer of the Yaquis.

In nurse's training, Laura had learned that the ancient Greeks, like the Yaquis, believed patients could be healed by dreams if they slept overnight in the Temple of Snakes. An odd coincidence or a faded memory of some lost truth?

Maya did her best to empty her mind so healing energy could flow unimpeded from her hands into Laura, energy to revive and strengthen Laura's own natural processes of healing so she could fight off the infection that threatened her life.

Maya wasn't conscious of time passing until the scrape of the opening door startled her. Recovering from her momentary disorientation, she scooped up the bracelet, slid it onto her arm and turned to see Robert staring at her.

"What in hell are you doing?" he asked.

"Laying on of hands," she told him as calmly as she could, using the term he'd be familiar with. "I believe it might help Laura." As she spoke, she straightened Laura and turned her onto her left side, propping her in that position with pillows.

He shrugged. "I suppose it's harmless enough."

Glancing at her watch, Maya was surprised to find thirty minutes had passed. She'd never before transferred energy for such a long time. Was that why she felt so drained?

Robert leaned over Laura and felt for her pulse. After a few moments he grunted and reached a hand to her eyelid. He started to lift the lid gently, intending, Maya knew, to check her pupil. Laura flinched, moving her head slightly to avoid his fingers.

A minimal response. Did it mean anything?

She caught the glint of hope in Robert's eyes when they met hers and they shared a moment of guarded optimism. He motioned with his head away from the bed, then walked to the window. She joined him.

"I'm glad you're here," he said quietly. "Sorry I snapped at you when I came in."

As she waved away the apology, she noted the stubble of beard across his jaw and the shadows under his eyes. How long had it been since he'd slept?

"Why don't you find a bed and sleep for an hour or so?" she asked.

He shook his head. "Not yet. Not until—" He didn't finish the sentence but he didn't need to.

Not until Laura improves.

"I napped at home," she told him. "You rest in the lounge chair."

After another brief exam of his sister, he eased into the chair, put his head back and closed his eyes. His confidence in her warmed Maya.

Just before one in the morning, as Maya was shifting Laura onto her back for a change in position, the girl moaned.

Instantly Robert was on his feet and at the bedside. "Laura." He spoke softly but urgently. "Laura, open your eyes."

The girl's blond lashes fluttered slowly and, as though it were difficult, she opened her eyes. It was clear to Maya that Laura didn't focus her eyes and they closed almost immediately. But the response made Maya's heart lift.

Robert looked up at Maya, relief brightening his expression. She smiled, understanding. Laura's increasing level of response encouraged them both.

By two, Laura opened her eyes spontaneously and made attempts to focus them, though she said nothing. A definite improvement.

"Why don't you try to sleep now?" Maya suggested, concerned by Robert's haggard look. "I'll call you if she doesn't continue to do well."

He nodded and put his hand on her shoulder. "Even if I don't agree with the laying of hands," he said, "I'll never forget what you've done for Laura." He bent and kissed her lightly, a mere brush of his lips on hers. Straightening, he smiled one-sidedly. "Just because I'm too tired for anything more right now doesn't mean you can trust me."

After he left the room, Maya lifted her fingers to her lips. She didn't understand how or why, but his brief caress had somehow infused her with renewed strength.

By the time Maya left at seven that morning, Laura was intermittently conscious and aware of her surroundings. Robert called Maya late that afternoon and told her he'd found a nurse for the night shift and that Laura was continuing to improve.

On Thursday, Laura went home.

"She's not quite back to normal," Robert told Maya in his clinic office on Friday morning. "She's too easily agitated—her pulse rate increases, her hands tremble, she cries. I think—I hope—it's a temporary nervous condition, caused by the brain inflammation. It should gradually subside."

"I'd like to visit her," Maya said.

He grimaced. "My mother's afraid to let anyone near Laura for fear she'll get overexcited. Not just you—she's turned away any number of Laura's friends. If she had her way she'd keep the poor kid flat on her back in bed—not a good idea."

Maya agreed. "You'll have to think of some way to break the pattern before Laura turns into a chronic invalid."

Robert eyed her speculatively. "How about a picnic this Sunday?"

"Great! Laura should enjoy being outdoors with you."

"And you."

"Me? But I—"

"You're good for her. I think she needs us both on that picnic."

Maya felt she couldn't refuse. Perhaps she'd be able to help Laura—she'd certainly like to try. And Robert would be no problem with his sister along.

"Let me bring the food," she offered.

He shook his head. "This is my picnic—I'll provide everything. All I need is you."

His gaze pinned her as helplessly in place as if she were nailed to the floor. As he brushed his forefinger across her lips, his words echoed in her head—need you, need you, need you.

"You'll be at the picnic for Laura," he said softly, "but you'll be there for me, too."

On Sunday morning, Robert helped his sister into her convertible, then slid behind the wheel. His sports car was not the car of choice for three people. He pulled away from the house, shaking his head when he noticed his mother peering anxiously from the screened porch. No matter how he'd tried to reassure her, she was positive the picnic would prove too strenuous for Laura.

"Like it feels really good to get out of the house," Laura said.

"Sure you haven't changed your mind about where you want to go?" he asked her, keeping his voice casual. He didn't want to upset his sister but he wished she'd chosen another spot.

"Nope. It's one of my favorite places and I haven't been there at all this summer. I'll bet *you* haven't been there in years."

"Wrong. I was there in May." If he couldn't change her mind, at least he could try to keep her quiet about where they were going. "I have an idea, Laura. Let's surprise Maya and not tell her beforehand where the picnic is to be, okay?"

"Some people don't like surprises. Does she?"

"I'm not sure. But let's try it."

Laura glanced sideways at him. "After you say her name you sort of pause, like you're listening to the sound of it."

"Maya's a pretty name," he said defensively, trying not to show she'd startled him.

"So is she. Pretty, I mean. When I saw her name on the party list I said to myself that I bet you told Mom to ask her." Laura sighed. "I guess Mom canceled the party altogether after I got sick."

"Postponed it anyway. I can't say I'm too unhappy."

"Me, either. Mom would never add the only person I really wanted to invite to her guest list. I couldn't even ask her 'cause she'd probably fire him or something gross like that."

Robert had no trouble guessing who she meant. "I don't think Sal wants to be asked."

Laura shifted to face him. "How do you know?" Her voice rose. "You say he's your friend but you never, ever, once asked him into our house. And you won't. 'Cause you're just as prejudiced as Mom. One thing about her—she doesn't pretend not to be."

Robert stared at her, jerking his eyes back to the road when the car began to drift. Laura spoke nonsense. He and Sal went back years. They'd been *compadres* since boyhood. He'd been to Sal's house dozens of times. Maybe hundreds. While it was true Sal hadn't been in the Pierson family home, that was because he hadn't wanted Sal to be patronized by his parents.

No, damn it, by his mother. His father, give the devil his due, wouldn't have treated Sal any differently than any other friend Robert brought home.

Prejudiced? Damned if he was!

Laura's sobbing brought his attention back to her. The last thing he wanted was to get her agitated. He reached over and squeezed her shoulder. "How about some nice soothing music from one of your favorite groups, Rush, maybe, or Mr. Big."

Laura sniffled. "Now you're making fun of my taste in music."

He put his hand over his heart. "Me? A man who grooved on XTC and Black Flag back in the golden rock days? Never!"

She hiccoughed and giggled. "You made those names up."

"I swear I didn't. Go ahead, pick a tape. Maybe you can convert me."

Flicking through the cassettes, she chose one and slid it in. "This is Hearts. They're like, different."

Different, he decided after the first stanza, was one description. Good God, was he getting old?

When Maya opened her door to his ring, he felt a be-ginning-to-be-familiar rush of pure joy at seeing her.

"You're staring at me," she said after a moment. "Did I forget to brush my hair?"

"Everything's fine," he said hastily. Everything except him.

He couldn't be near Maya without wanting to touch her. Hold her. If Laura wasn't waiting in the car... But today belonged to Laura and he meant to keep that firmly in mind. If he could. Considering where they were headed, he doubted it.

"You were there in the hospital with me, weren't you?" Laura asked Maya after they greeted each other.

In the back seat, Maya buckled her seat belt before replying. "I was your nurse the first night."

"Robert said you were. I thought I'd just dreamed about you, you know?"

"I was really there."

"In the silver rain," Laura said softly.

"What are you talking about?" Robert demanded as he backed the convertible from Maya's drive.

"My dream," Laura said. "Like, I was in this place and the sun was blazing down and I couldn't move. You know, like the grapevines are staked and wired? That's how I felt. Trapped. Burning up. Then Maya came and this silver rain began to fall—you know, like a sprinkler got turned on.

"The rain was cool and wonderful and when it fell on me it freed me. After that everything got confused and I wasn't sure if I was dreaming or awake. When I woke up all the way, Maya wasn't there."

Robert's half-questioning, half-skeptical gaze met Maya's in the rearview mirror for a moment before she looked away. She'd like to believe Laura's silver rain had been the healing energy she'd transferred but she knew better than to mention such a possibility to him.

"I'm happy you're doing so well," Maya told Laura.

Laura turned to look at her. "Mom doesn't think so, does she, Rob?" Her voice held a note of uncertainty, as though she weren't convinced she was recovering.

"She's being overprotective," he said. "You know how mothers are. You're doing great—otherwise I wouldn't be taking you on this picnic." He reached over and tousled her hair. "Don't tell me you thought I was feeding you a last meal!"

She grinned at him. "Well, you *did* ask where I wanted to eat the meal. You never bothered to before." Laura glanced back at Maya. "It's a surprise. Where we're going, I mean."

"I can hardly wait," Maya said.

"I'll bet Maya will like Hearts," Laura said, and turned on the tape deck. Music blasted out.

Today's music didn't grip Maya, not the way the music of her own teenage years had; she could take or leave it. She smiled at Laura and let the sound flow past her, enjoying it in a relaxed way, much as she enjoyed the rush of the warm wind through her hair.

It was fun riding in a convertible. She couldn't really equate the ride with being on a horse but she found similarities.

Not until Robert turned onto the dirt track leading onto Pierson property did she have any inkling where they might be headed. She tensed as the car jounced over the uneven road, not so much from the bouncing as from the realization of what Laura's choice must be.

No, she thought. I can't go there. Not with him.

Since she could hardly leap from the car or demand Robert stop and let her out, Maya gritted her teeth. For Laura's sake, she'd do her best to pretend nothing was amiss. If she could.

The track deteriorated, forcing him to stop short of their destination. "If we don't want broken springs, I guess I'll have to carry you the rest of the way, Sis," he said.

"I can walk," Laura protested.

Maya stared at the sycamores, at their thick white-gray trunks, splotched with brown, at the spreading branches whose leaves fluttered in the breeze. A red-winged blackbird called an accompaniment to an unseen woodpecker drilling for his dinner. Very faintly, the stream murmured to her, promising coolness, promising her heart's delight as it had long ago....

Belatedly she realized Robert had spoken and she turned to him in confusion. "What?"

"I asked if you could manage the blanket and picnic basket," he said.

"Yes. Yes, of course."

She was glad to have something to distract her from rerunning the past through her mind like an old and disturbing movie.

Laura did walk part of the way but Robert insisted on carrying her when her steps lagged. Maya trailed them, doing her best to concentrate on the present, on making the picnic a success. For Laura.

But no matter how she tried, when she stepped under the shade of the sycamores, her breath caught. Let's stop here, she wanted to say. Let's not go any farther. But her throat was too dry for words.

And so they came to the moon pool.

Maya placed blanket, pillow and basket on the ground and stepped to the bank, staring down into the swirling water trapped by the boulders. The stream was lower than it had been in May but the pool was still there. Shaded by the interlacing tree branches, the water held a seductive invitation.

"I wish I'd brought my swimsuit," Laura said.

"One thing at a time," Robert told her.

"*You* don't think I'm better, either." Laura's voice held a trace of petulance.

"You're doing fine," he said, "but I'm your doctor as well as your brother and doctors are notoriously conservative. Isn't that right, Maya?"

She turned to look at him, still bemused by the pool. His gaze held hers and the question in his eyes had nothing to do with what he'd asked her in words.

Maya took a deep breath and forced herself to glance away. Focusing on Laura, she said, "Conservative Dr. Pierson can't object to us taking our shoes off and dangling our feet in the water."

Laura rolled her eyes. "I guess that's better than nothing."

Minutes later, Maya and Laura sat side by side on the creek bank with their bare feet cooling in the water.

"Have you seen Sal lately?" Laura asked, her voice carefully casual.

"He stopped by yesterday evening while he was exercising Padrino," Maya said.

"He brought me some fresh picked apricots earlier and I'm sure he wanted to see me but Mom wouldn't let him in." Laura turned to face Maya. "It isn't fair! No one wants me and Sal to be together."

Maya decided that the longer Laura wrapped herself in her fantasy of a romance with Sal, the harder it would be for the girl to face the truth. Considering Laura's convalescent state, she'd have to be careful what she said, but the fantasy had gone far enough. What was the matter with her cousin that he hadn't nipped this thing in the bud?

"Sal told me that he felt like your big brother," Maya said. "I'm sure he's concerned about you."

Laura's eyes widened. "I don't believe you!"

"Laura," Robert said. "Maya's telling the truth."

Laura sprang to her feet. "You two are conspiring against Sal and me, just like Mom is." Her voice rose and she began to tremble. "You don't want us to be together. Rob thinks because I'm a Pierson I can't fall in love with a Chicano, that he's beneath me. And, Maya, you want Sal for yourself so you—"

"Laura!" Robert's voice snapped like a whip.

She burst into tears.

Maya, on her feet, put an arm around Laura's quivering shoulders and propelled her to the blanket Robert had spread under a tree. She eased her down until Laura's head was on her shoulder, and held her, murmuring soothingly.

As Laura's sobs began to ebb, Maya said, "Do you remember how you dreamed about silver rain?"

When Laura made a sound that might have been agreement, Maya handed her a tissue and she wiped her eyes with shaking hands.

"Stretch out and put your head in my lap," Maya said softly but with an undercurrent of firmness.

Laura hesitated, sniffling, then obeyed.

"Close your eyes," Maya ordered.

When Laura did, Maya placed her hands, one over the other, on the girl's forehead. "Think of rain," she said in a gentle singsong. "Silver rain, cool and refreshing, rain that showers through your head, filtering down, down, down, deep into your body. Silver rain that cleanses, silver rain that heals." Her voice grew softer, slower, as she repeated the words over and over.

Laura gradually relaxed, her tremors stopped, her breathing grew deeper and more regular.

Finally, Maya slid Laura's head onto the pillow and stood looking down at the girl. When she was satisfied that Laura slept, she stepped off the blanket and walked back to the pool. Though she didn't so much as glance at him, she knew Robert followed her.

He took her hand and pulled her away from the pool, deeper into the trees, farther from Laura. She didn't resist. In calming Laura she'd depleted her own energy, and whether she liked it or not, whether she understood the reason or not, she knew his touch could restore her quickly and completely. She wished that was the only reason she longed to feel his arms around her.

He stopped and put his hands on her shoulders, forcing her to look at him.

"I didn't want to come here," he said.

"Nor I."

"I have to hold you." His voice thickened, grew hoarse. "Do you understand?"

She nodded, past words, and flowed into his arms, pressing her cheek to his chest. The regular, comforting thub-dub of his heart quickened under her ear. Her own pulse rate doubled and she raised her head. His eyes, pupils dilated by need, stared into hers.

"I can't help how I feel," he whispered, and his lips covered hers.

She clung to him, savoring his taste, like no other man's, inhaling his remembered scent, an aphrodisiac more potent than any potion of legend. He pulled her closer, fitting her against him as the kiss deepened.

Eleven years had done nothing to diminish the power he had to liquefy her bones as her synapses sizzled and crackled with the fiery messages they carried to every cell in her body. No matter that a little warning voice in her head muttered that he was Robert Pierson and he wasn't for her—he was exactly what she'd always wanted.

Evident as his desire was, she sensed his restraint. A man held her, not the boy of eleven years ago. Just as she was not the naive girl but a woman who recognized her own unfulfilled need. For him. No other man would do. The realization unnerved her.

He broke the kiss but continued to hold her, his lips brushing hers.

"It's still there," he whispered, "still between us. We're damn well trapped."

"Yes." Her word was almost a moan.

"I can't get free. You haunt me."

Feeling his warm breath on her face, taking the air he'd breathed into her lungs, excited her almost beyond bearing. But it wasn't enough. She wanted more. More than kisses and caresses. More than being held. She wanted what this man alone could give her. And yet...

"I'm afraid," she whispered.

He groaned. "I never meant to hurt you."

Hadn't he? Maya stiffened, remembering.

He swore under his breath and let her go.

"This place is cursed," he said.

Maya managed a smile as shaky as her knees felt as she stepped back. "Maybe it's us."

He shook his head. "It can't be you. You're not cursed. If anything you're blessed. After what I just saw you do for Laura, you're forcing me to rethink this laying on of hands. Old Gonzalez calls you *La Curandera* and swears you, not I, cured the sore on his foot. Since he 'forgot' to take the antibiotic I gave him, he may even be right. What did you give him to put in the hot soaks?"

She bit her lip. "You agreed that I could give him a mild antiseptic for the soaks. So I stuffed a few potassium permanganate crystals in several packets. I thought if the water turned purple he might be convinced he was being cured. But I certainly don't take any credit for—"

Robert chuckled. "The power of suggestion?"

She smiled reluctantly, uneasy with the name Mr. Gonzalez had called her. "I do believe in healing energy and I may use what my grandfather taught me to augment my own energy, but I'm a nurse, not a folk healer."

"Is augmenting what you were doing here that night in May?" He nodded his head toward the pool but kept his gaze fixed on her.

Maya flushed, looking away. He caught her face gently between his fingers and made her turn to him again.

"I've never seen anyone more beautiful in my life." Robert's voice thrilled through her. "I never expect to."

He bent his head and her lips parted as his mouth came down on hers. She forgot everything. Nothing existed except their kiss. As far as she was concerned it could go on forever....

"Caught you!" Laura called, half laughing, half accusing.

Chapter Eight

Maya parked her VW in the graveled area near the Pierson stables and slid from the car. She hesitated. Her elderly bug was the only one of its kind among an array of new and expensive cars. She feared she'd be equally out of place at the party.

Laura had told her at one of their twice-a-week healing sessions that her mother had finally given in to her pleas and agreed to have the party after all.

"Like, I think she decided she'd rather have the party than keep listening to me," Laura said. "Besides, it's been three weeks since I got out of the hospital. Anyone can see I'm not sick anymore."

Laura had been one of the lucky patients. In the Thompsonville area, four had died and at least two were left with permanent brain damage from the encephalitis epidemic.

The past three weeks had been hectic in the clinic and as bad or worse, Maya was sure, for Robert on the weekends. Now, thanks to the efforts of the mosquito control district, cases were tapering off.

Maya looked up at the waxing crescent moon sliding down the deep blue evening sky toward the western horizon, close to setting. She took a deep breath of the warm night breeze, tinged with the earthy scent of horses as well as the sweet aroma of the star jasmine climbing the grape-stake fence separating the parking area from the stable, corral and barn. Music and laughter drifting from the patio on the opposite side of the house beckoned her.

Time to face the enemy. If the party guests weren't her enemy, Susan Pierson was. She'd continued to fight Laura's visits to Maya even after Robert had conceded that Maya's laying on of hands was helping the girl.

It's not what I do, Maya thought. It's what I am. Or, maybe, *who* I am. But she invited me to this party. I've come this far and I'm going the rest of the way.

She began to walk slowly toward the house.

Robert saw Maya before she reached the brick path leading between the oleanders to the patio. Dressed in white, she seemed to float toward him—*una paloma blanca*. No, not *a* white dove. His. That much he was sure of. She had to be his. He started toward her.

They met among the oleanders, surrounded by white and pink blossoms that gave off no discernible fragrance. It flitted through his mind that oleanders were poisonous. But not to look at or to smell. Just to taste.

He took her hands, stopping her. Even in the dim light he could see how lovely she looked in the long white gown. Her cloud of dark hair was caught up on one side with a silver clasp; otherwise she wore no ornament except for the ever-present silver bracelet.

He gazed at her, wanting to say to hell with the party and lead her away from the crowd. He longed to be alone with her. They'd hardly had a chance to speak to each other these past few weeks unless it was about a patient.

"Hello, Robert," she said softly.

"Maya, I'm glad you're here. I thought you—"

"Might not come?" She shook her head. "I was invited. I came." She tugged her hands free. "Shall we go on?"

As they emerged onto the lighted brick patio, he noticed speculative looks from the older guests and smiled, tucking her arm into his. Let them wonder. He led her across to his mother.

"I believe you two have met," he said.

Susan Pierson inclined her head stiffly. "Ms. Najero. So glad you could come." Her tone belied her welcome.

"It was kind of you to ask me, Mrs. Pierson." Maya's voice was as formal as her words.

"Maya!" Laura waved from a lounge chair by the pool. "Over here."

Maya nodded politely to his mother, smiled briefly at him and strolled toward his sister.

"She looks like her," his mother half whispered.

Robert wasn't quite certain of her meaning. "What?"

Susan drew him apart from the guests. "Did you know I saw Estella Gabaldon only once?" she asked.

"Maya's mother?"

Susan nodded. "You were about two and had been left home with the maid while your father and I drove into town. He noticed Caesar Gabaldon sitting in his truck along the main street, parked and got out to tell the old man something. You know your father's deplorable habit of treating some of his workers like they were his friends."

"I suppose he felt they *were* friends." Robert was surprised by his own words—he'd never before in his life defended his father. He couldn't remember how young he'd been when he'd first sided with his mother but his loyalty to her had never wavered. She was right, his father wrong.

Susan didn't seem to notice his momentary deflection. "I waited in the car. And so I saw her first, coming out of Olstrom's Department Store. Her body was distorted by far-advanced pregnancy, her face drawn and her long black hair tied back with a twist of ribbon. Yet when your father caught sight of her, he couldn't look away. He left old Caesar and hurried to her side. They were close enough so I could hear every word." Susan caught her lip between her teeth.

"'I thought you were in Mexico,' your father said. She told him her husband had been killed and she'd come back to live with her father. Neither of them said another word. But they stood on the sidewalk in front of Olstrom's for what seemed hours, the pair of them staring at each other. Staring and staring. Until her father called her name." Susan glanced at Robert. "I knew then George had never loved me and he never would. Not as he did her."

The sad little story made Robert feel almost as much sympathy for Estella and his father as he did for his mother. All three had been hurt. He touched his mother's arm. "I'm sorry."

"Yet you insisted on inviting her daughter here."

"Maya isn't her mother."

"She carries Gabaldon blood."

Robert looked his mother full in the face. "Maya is not her mother. Estella Gabaldon is a ghost who belongs in the past. The living shouldn't invoke ghosts. They should allow the past to rest in peace."

Even as he spoke, he knew his own past still haunted him. How could he blame his mother?

Susan gazed at him for a long moment. Then, without saying a word, she walked away to greet new arrivals.

Robert looked for Maya but she was not with Laura and her friends beside the pool. He finally saw her near the combo, laughing with one of the guitar players. Irrational anger seethed in his gut as he strode toward her.

A pretty blonde in a pale blue sundress stopped him halfway, threw her arms around him and kissed him enthusiastically. "Robbie! This is the first time I've seen you all summer. Don't tell me that old clinic keeps you that busy."

"Hello, Julie," he said, stepping back. "Actually I *have* been busy. I didn't even realize you were home."

She pouted. He might have found the pout charming when they were both twenty but it irritated him now.

"It's been a year since my divorce and I've been here all that time." Julie sounded a bit irritated herself.

"Once I moved to San Francisco, I'm afraid I stopped keeping up with the local news," he said. "Please excuse me, I must talk to someone."

He could tell Julie wasn't pleased to be left. Though they'd had a brief fling before her marriage to a Los Angeles lawyer, whatever had attracted him to her then didn't now. All he could think of was finding Maya.

To his annoyance, the combo had resumed playing and Maya was nowhere to be seen. He scanned the crowd and saw her dancing with a tall, thin teenager who he realized must be one of his sister's friends. From the bemused look on the guy's face, he'd forgotten anyone existed except Maya.

Robert cut in ruthlessly, murmuring, "She's too old for you, kid."

"I enjoyed dancing with you, Lenny," Maya called as Robert swung her away.

"Not half as much as he did with you," Robert told her. "Who's the guitar player you were talking to?"

"Someone I knew in high school. He told me their group is on the verge of a real break. They have a gig coming up in L.A. that might lead to a record contract. Isn't that great?"

Robert managed to grunt an answer, struggling with his anger as he wondered if the damn guitarist had ever made love to Maya. He shook his head, dismayed by the first serious attack of jealousy he'd ever felt.

Since he didn't intend to let her out of his arms, they danced to every number, Robert hoping for one with a slow beat so he'd have an excuse to hold her closer. It didn't happen; the combo took a break before playing one. On purpose? he wondered.

He led her to the bar set up under one of the oaks. She chose tonic water with lime; he asked for vodka in his. As they sipped their drinks, Robert maneuvered her carefully through the throng, changing direction whenever anyone seemed about to greet either of them.

"What changed Laura's mind about the party?" Maya asked when they were sitting side by side on a canopied garden swing at the far end of the patio. "At the picnic she said she was glad it had been canceled."

He frowned. "I'm not sure what goes on in her devious little mind. Laura's been a game-player since the day she learned her first word. I may love my kid sister but I'm on to her, believe me. Eventually the reason she changed her mind will surface and no one will be happy about it except Laura.''

"Come on, she's a sweet kid.''

"You haven't known her long enough. Bright, yes. Loyal, yes. Stubborn, yes. Honest, yes, if it suits her. Otherwise she can't be trusted. Sweet, no way.'' He swallowed the rest of his drink and set the glass on a wrought-iron table.

"Do you miss San Francisco?'' she asked.

"Not much.'' He thought of telling her how he'd begun to chafe at his predictable, well-channeled life in the city and decided this wasn't the time or the place for confessions. For that, they needed to be alone. For that and for other, more urgent reasons.

"I love the Valley.'' Maya spoke dreamily. "This is where I was born. My home.''

Remembering his mother's story, he said, "You were almost born in Mexico, weren't you?'' As soon as the words were out, he wished them back.

He felt her tense and took her glass from her, setting it aside. He clasped both her hands in his. "We can't keep circling around what we both know about the past. But I admit I shouldn't have brought up the subject in public. Come into the house with me and we'll find a quiet place to talk.''

She shook her head. ''I was invited to a party.'' She pulled her hands free and gestured. "This is the party. Besides, I promised Laura I'd come back and talk to her. She claims her mother won't let her dance more than once every half hour and she's bored to tears.''

"Mother's still fretting over her. Unreasonable as it is, she blames herself for letting Laura get sick.''

"Laura's doing really well with the energy imagery—it's a wonderful self-healing tool. She's learned to bring what she calls the silver rain by herself. She'll be fine." Maya rose from the swing.

Robert stood up, too. "Okay, first we talk to Laura. Then *we* talk. No arguments."

But Laura wasn't on the lounge where she'd been earlier. She wasn't among the dancers or anywhere in sight.

"Maybe she went inside," Robert said. "Come on, we'll take a look."

Maya hesitated, then followed him. A few of the older guests had drifted into the air-conditioned house and were seated in the living room, talking. Laura was not with them. Robert was about to leave Maya in the library and search upstairs when the phone rang. Used to most calls being for him, he picked it up.

"Dr. Pierson here."

"Rob, thank God you answered."

"Sal? Is that you?"

"Yeah. Look, Laura's over here at my place and she's pretty beat. I can bring her back in the pickup but how the hell can I explain that her coming here wasn't my idea. Not mine in any way, shape or form."

"So *that's* the reason," Robert said.

"What?"

"Never mind. I'll bring Maya. We're on our way." As he hung up and turned to Maya, his beeper went off.

The hospital had an emergency.

Maya drove to Sal's alone. To her surprise, Laura's convertible wasn't in his drive. How had she gotten there?

"Damn little fool rode over on her mare," Sal told her a few minutes later. "I'll return the horse in the morning—just get that kid out of my house. Pronto!"

Maya eyed Sal, bare-chested, barefoot, wearing denim cutoffs and the most horrendous scowl she'd ever seen. "Calm down, cuz," she advised.

Laura was curled on Sal's frayed corduroy couch, looking fragile and stubborn at the same time.

"I'm not going home," she announced.

Maya opened her mouth to try reasoning, but Sal, elbowing her aside, slung Laura over his shoulder and marched from the house, dumping the girl into the passenger seat of the VW. "And don't come back," he said as he slammed the door.

Before Maya had turned the ignition key, he was gone. "I'd say that was a bit stronger than a hint," she said as she pulled from the drive. "Whatever possessed you to ride over here?"

The silence lasted so long she thought Laura didn't mean to answer and was surprised when the girl finally muttered, "'Cause I wanted to see Sal."

"At night? Uninvited?"

Laura sat up straighter. "Well, how could I get to see him if not tonight when the party's on? Mom never takes her eyes off me. I had to distract her somehow."

Maybe devious *was* a more descriptive word for Laura than sweet.

"Does Rob know?" Laura asked.

"You bet he does. The only reason he's not with me is because he got an emergency call."

Laura sighed. "He's going to yell at me."

"I'm afraid you deserve it."

"You don't understand."

"I understand Sal didn't want you there."

"He may be your cousin but you don't know zip about Sal. He *does* want me, only he's got all these, like, old-fashioned hang-ups about protecting innocent young girls. Like, I try to get across to him I'm not that young or that innocent but—" She paused, shrugging her shoulders. "He's one stubborn male."

"I'd give it up if I were you."

Laura slanted a look at her. "Would you give up my brother without doing everything you could think of first?"

Maya, taken aback, couldn't find a ready answer. "Robert and I aren't really involved," she said finally. "Not the way you think."

Laura snorted. "You must have the idea I'm stupid or something. At that picnic the two of you forgot not only me but the rest of the world. Don't give me any 'just friends' crap. He got Mom to ask you to the party—and for some reason she doesn't much care for you, as I guess you know." Laura patted Maya's arm. "*I* like you. Besides, you're good for Rob. My brother was turning into a big city honcho—he needed someone to stand him on his head and shake him until some of the stuffing came out."

Maya couldn't help chuckling at the image. "I can't take any credit for that."

"Sure you can. 'Cause you've got him going in circles. Nobody ever did that to Rob before. The girls around here sort of swooned into his arms if he looked at them. You, you're a challenge to him. Like Sal is to me."

For Laura, everything ultimately came back to Sal. Maya wondered what the girl would do next. Once at Stanford, she believed Laura's infatuation with Sal would fade—but September was a month away.

"I don't think your game playing is good for either you or Sal," she told Laura.

"Game playing?" Laura's voice rose. "You think I don't mean what I say? I love Sal. He loves me, too, only the trouble is he can't see past those fourteen years separating us. If I could somehow, just once, get him into bed—"

"No, that's a mistake. Besides being definitely unwise, you'd be setting a trap. Being dishonest."

"I love Sal so anything's fair."

Maya shook her head. "If there's no honesty between a man and woman, how can there be love?"

When Laura said nothing, Maya was forced to listen to her own words echoing in her head. She'd once mistakenly thought there was love between her and Robert. Had there ever been honesty? Was honesty between them now?

"What if Sal finds someone else while I'm at Stanford?" Laura said at last.

"Haven't you considered the possibility *you* might find someone?"

"How can I find someone when Sal's the one?"

"So, all right, if he believes you're the one for him, then he'll wait for you to grow up a little more. If you're wrong about how he feels, he won't wait. But that would mean he never did feel for you what you've decided you feel for him, so it was no go from the beginning."

Laura clutched Maya's arm. "I'm scared to take the chance. I can't bear the thought of losing him."

Maya took a deep breath and let it out slowly. "Laura, you don't have him, not really." Not any more than I have Robert, she added silently.

Laura's sigh sounded as though it came from her toes. "But I do. We're, like, bound, you know? Only he won't face the truth. Maybe it's 'cause I'm a Pierson." Her voice turned plaintive. "That doesn't matter to me. Why should it to him?"

Her talk of binding made Maya uneasy. Laura's fantasy about Sal was far more elaborate and deep-rooted than Maya had dreamed it could be. He'd allowed this to go on much too long. She and Sal were overdue to have a serious talk.

Whether Laura admitted it or not, the fact she was a Pierson *did* matter. Certainly to her mother and most probably to Sal, too. To protect him, Maya decided she wouldn't, even if asked directly, tell Susan Pierson where she'd found Laura.

As if reading her mind, Laura asked, "Do you have to tell my mother where I was?"

"No, I'll leave that up to you."

Though she hoped against hope Laura's absence had gone unnoticed, Maya wasn't surprised when she saw Susan waiting by the driveway when the VW pulled in.

"Oh, oh," Laura muttered. "I'm in trouble."

She waited until Maya got out and came around to open her door. "You can lean on me," Maya offered, feeling Laura tremble.

"No, I'm okay. Really."

Maya walked with her to be sure. They both stopped before reaching Susan.

"I might have known you were at the bottom of this," Susan snapped, glaring at Maya.

"Mom, she had nothing to do—"

"I'm not speaking to you, Laura."

"But Maya didn't—"

"Please be quiet!" Susan didn't raise her voice but it held a razor's edge. "Laura, you will go into the house immediately and upstairs to your room. I'll talk to you later."

Laura shot Maya an apologetic glance and went in through the front door. Tamping down her anger, Maya willed herself to calmness, her chin rising as she faced Susan.

"Ms. Najero, I don't know if this is your idea of a joke or if you set out to deliberately harm Laura but I find your behavior despicable. I cannot imagine why you'd—" A loud screech of brakes stopped her.

Both women turned to look.

Robert jumped from the car, leaving the door open, and strode toward them.

"Laura?" he asked.

"She's fine," Maya put in hastily.

"I sent her to her room," Susan said. "I'm now waiting for an explanation from Ms. Najero."

"I have no explanation that you'd be willing to accept, Mrs. Pierson." Maya spoke crisply. "If you'll excuse me, it's past time I left."

Robert put a hand on her arm. "Maya, wait. What's this all about?"

Maya had used up her entire store of reasonableness. If she didn't get away from here in a hurry her fury was going to erupt and she was damned if she'd lose her cool in front of Mrs. Pierson.

"Ask your mother!" she cried, pulling free and running to her car. Gravel showered behind her as she shot from the drive.

She drove straight to Sal's and hammered on his closed door. He flung it open.

Maya marched inside before she turned on him. "Just what kind of a game are you playing with Laura?" she demanded, her anger freed from restraint. "Why in hell didn't you stop this before it got out of control?"

He held up his hands. "Easy, cuz, easy. I don't play games, not me."

She stared at him. "*Are* you in love with her, then?"

Sal grimaced. "That's one hell of a question. In love with a kid young enough to be my daughter?"

"Your daughter? Not unless you were a lot more precocious than I heard at the time. Fourteen years does not a generation make. Answer the question straight. All I ever hear from you are evasions."

"Like a brother, maybe," Sal said after a short silence.

"You love Laura like a brother. Maybe."

"Okay, then, like a brother."

"You don't feel 'bound' to her?"

Sal blinked. "What's that supposed to mean?"

"That you and she are fated to love. Kismet."

He opened his mouth and closed it without speaking. Twice. Maya's eyes narrowed. Why wasn't he laughing at her. Why wasn't he telling her she was *mucho loca?* She and Laura both.

"Ah, hell, she's too young to know what she wants," he muttered at last. "With her father dead and Rob gone, Laura got fixed on me because she needed a man she could count on. When she decided she was in love with me, what was I supposed to do? Tell the poor kid to get lost?"

Maya frowned. "I'm beginning to wonder if Laura isn't right," she said slowly. "Maybe she knows you better than you know yourself."

"Come on, she's just a kid. She'll go off to Stanford, meet some guy who's her kind and forget all these crazy ideas about me."

"And will you forget the feeling you have for her?"

He scowled. "Hey, cuz, some things are private, you know? You and Rob have a thing going, haven't you? How'd you like me to ask you if you're in love with him?"

Maya clutched her hands together as his words settled into her head. In love? With Robert?

"Hit home, did I?" Sal asked.

She couldn't be in love with the man she'd hated for eleven years. No, impossible!

"Lots of luck, cuz," Sal said. "Rob's okay but don't forget he's a Pierson."

And Susan Pierson hated her. Maya swallowed, fighting back tears. Not love. It couldn't be love.

"If it's any help," Sal added, "I'd say Rob's in love with you. Just don't ask me if he can admit it—he's got some hang-ups that go way back."

Honesty. How could there be love without honesty? Despite her efforts, tears gathered in Maya's eyes.

"Oh, hell," Sal said, putting an arm around her shoulders. "I didn't mean to make you feel bad."

The moment she felt his comforting touch, the dam burst. Maya put her head against Sal's chest and wept. Angry tears, because of Susan. Sad tears for Laura and for Sal. Desperate and confused tears because she didn't know what to do about her feelings for Robert.

Sal's arms came around her and he patted her back, murmuring soothing words. She cried harder.

Robert stood on Sal's porch, staring in through the screen, his fists clenching at the sight of Maya in Sal's arms. She'd fled from him and come straight to Sal.

After a delay in calming down his mother, setting her straight and then making certain Laura was all right, he'd driven to Maya's place. Her car wasn't there so he'd come here to talk to Sal.

And here she was. In Sal's arms. He reminded himself they were cousins but that didn't help much. What hurt was that she'd turned to someone else for comfort. Why hadn't it been to him?

Robert started away from the door, stopped. No, he was here; he'd have his say.

"Am I interrupting?" He'd meant to ask the question coolly but the words held a sharp edge, betraying his confused emotions.

Sal looked over Maya's shoulder at him. "Come on in, Rob," he said. "Maya's kind of upset."

Robert hesitated, then opened the screen door. Maya pushed away from Sal and, face averted, started into the kitchen. He followed, took her arm, turned her toward him, saw her face was wet with tears and began to put his arms around her.

"Leave me alone!" She jerked free and slammed out the back door.

"I think you'd better listen up," Sal advised. "Maya can't take any more tonight."

As Robert tried to make up his mind what to do, he heard the VW pull from Sal's driveway. He could trail her to her apartment but, considering his mother's unjust accusations, Maya had a right to be angry. Angry enough so he doubted if she'd let him in. Giving up for the time being, he returned to the living room and flung himself onto the couch. He had another matter to straighten out.

"Mind telling me what's going on with you and Laura?" he asked Sal.

Sal's smile was without humor. "First things first. You saw how upset Maya was—my cousin doesn't cry easily. I think you'd better tell me what's going on between you and Maya.''

Robert stared at him. His initial reaction—that it was none of Sal's business—gave way to the realization that he didn't have a ready answer. What *was* between him and Maya?

Chapter Nine

Too upset to sleep, Maya spent several restless hours in bed. Finally she removed her silver bracelet and held it between her hands, willing her mind into blankness, evicting all thoughts of Robert. Eventually she drifted off.

He stood on a hill above her, both arms stretched wide at shoulder height, the sun rising behind him, his blond hair blowing in the morning breeze. Grapevines, staked to T-bars, grew around him, branches and tendrils entwining him, reaching to his waist. After a moment she saw with horror why his arms were outstretched. He, like the vines, was staked. Helpless.

His lips moved, calling to her, she knew, though she couldn't hear his voice.

"I'm coming!" she tried to shout, but her words died unborn.

She attempted to climb the hill, only to find that a silver barrier encircled her, rising higher and higher as she tried to get over it until at last the encircling ring towered above her head, blotting him from sight. She was as trapped as he.

They were separated forever.

Maya woke with the dawn breeze blowing through her window and an ache in her heart. The dream haunted her while she sipped orange juice, then accompanied her like a ghost into the shower. Dream shards still clung disturbingly to her mind as she donned white shorts and a red-and-white-checked halter made from cotton table napkins.

She brushed her hair more vigorously than usual, as if hoping to brush away the dream, the bracelet loosening and sliding down her arm to her wrist. Absently she pushed it higher and froze, her hand on the cool silver.

A silver barrier. A silver bracelet. That could hardly be coincidence—but what did it mean?

She shook her head, slid her feet into thong sandals, ran down the steps and out into the already warm morning. She walked through the grove, the trees heavy with green oranges, to the hill she'd often climbed. At the bottom, she paused. For some reason, one she couldn't identify, she didn't want to climb the hill today.

Suspecting her reluctance had something to do with her dream, she tried to force herself to go up but found she could not. She turned at last and wandered through the grove again, settling into a webbed lounge chair under the large Modesto ash tree at the back of the house.

When she closed her eyes an image of Robert's face formed in the darkness behind her lids. No matter what, she couldn't escape him, couldn't escape thinking about him, dreaming about him. He'd become more important than anything or anyone else.

She couldn't be in love with Robert. How could she possibly be so foolish as to make the same mistake her mother had made all those years ago? He was a Pierson, she was a Gabaldon-Najero. To love him was hopeless, as hopeless as Laura's infatuation with Sal.

Maya sighed, opening her eyes. What she felt was no mere infatuation. No matter that she was foolish, she might as well admit the truth—she was in love—with Robert.

Had the dream been trying to warn her of the hopelessness of it all? Somehow she thought there'd been more meaning to the dream but what it was escaped her.

Last night Sal had said he thought Robert was in love with her. Though she was well aware that Robert wanted her, she didn't believe his interest went any further—just as it hadn't eleven years ago. She'd thought she was in love with him then; she knew she was now.

So, okay, she'd admitted the uncomfortable truth. She'd made the same mistake all over again. What could she do about it? The wisest course would be never to see him again but that was clearly impossible. She couldn't leave the clinic in the lurch. She'd just have to hang on until Joe Halago returned and Robert left.

If she could somehow manage not to see Robert except at work, she might—

She froze, listening. A car was turning in the drive. She recognized the sound of the motor—Robert's car. Maya fought an impulse to flee. No. She wasn't a coward.

He'd said last night they must talk. So talk they would. Nothing else. Regardless of how she felt, she had no intention of falling into his arms. Rising from the chair, she stalked warily around the house.

"I thought you'd never let me set foot inside your apartment," Robert told her a few minutes later as he stood in her living room, looking around. "I really like those Indian prints. Yaqui, like the bracelet?"

She nodded, pleased that he'd remembered.

"Would you like some orange juice?" she asked. "I picked all the ripe Valencias right after I moved in so they wouldn't go to waste, squeezed them and froze the juice. I've got a freezer full. It might not be exactly fresh squeezed out but it was personally squeezed."

"That's sure to improve the taste. Actually I haven't had breakfast."

Neither had she; she hadn't felt like eating. "I don't have any eggs but I can offer you oatmeal-raisin bread, toasted, and coffee."

"Sounds good to me."

He followed her into the kitchen, hovering over her while she poured the orange juice, making her heart pound and her breath catch, making her forget that all she meant to do was talk to him. She thrust the glass into his hand and pointed firmly to the dinette area. "Sit!"

As he obeyed, his smile told her he knew very well he was distracting her.

By the time she sat across from him at the small table, she was more in command of herself. He wore a faded blue tank top that revealed more of him than she wanted to cope with. Luckily the table hid what was left bare by his white shorts.

Noticing the beeper at his waist, she said, "Do you actually show up at the hospital dressed like that?"

"In the shorts, yes, but I admit I leave a shirt in the car. I wouldn't want the home folks to think of a La Raza Clínica doctor as scruffy."

No one would ever call him scruffy. He was so good to look at that her gaze drifted back to him no matter how much she willed herself not to stare.

"You came to talk, I believe," she said.

He smiled. "Can't talk while I'm eating. Never had oatmeal-raisin toast before. It's great. Doesn't even need jelly. You also make good coffee. Not to mention the sort-of-fresh-squeezed orange juice. Come on, try the toast. Otherwise I'll feel like a glutton."

Maya had never felt less like eating but, not wanting him to realize he affected her so strongly, she broke off a piece of toast and put it in her mouth.

"Not that it's easy to eat with you sitting across from me," he added. "That's an interesting use for table napkins."

Feeling his gaze on her breasts made her nipples peak. She was afraid the napkin halter didn't hide the evidence but she could hardly cross her arms over her chest.

"Finish your toast." Though his voice gave nothing away, she caught the wicked gleam in his eye. He knew exactly what he'd done to her.

She choked down the rest of the toast with the aid of coffee, pushed her plate away and said, "Let's get to what you came here to talk about."

"Not across a table." He finished the last piece of toast, drained his cup, rose and reached a hand to help her up.

Avoiding his touch, she stood, but found him too close. "We can talk in the living room," she said, hastily moving away from him. "It's pretty warm in there so if you'll close the windows, I'll turn on the air-conditioning."

"I think we'll need it," he told her.

She didn't find his words reassuring.

Maya preferred the couch but chose a chair to be on the safe side. No way did she want the distraction of sitting next to Robert. He picked the couch, crossing one leg at a right angle over the other. His legs were covered with golden hair all the way up to where his muscular thighs disappeared into his white shorts. Why she should find that erotic she had no idea.

"I wanted to follow you home last night," he said, "but Sal persuaded me you needed to be alone."

"He was right."

"I'm sorry my mother misread Laura's escapade."

"Misread?" Maya stiffened. "Perhaps. I'm quite aware your mother doesn't like me."

Robert waved a hand. "It's not you she's unhappy with, it's her past. You and I have a past, too, and that's what we have to talk about. What happened to us then. Because it's affecting what's between us now as well as what could be between us."

Maya sat straighter, feeling threatened. "What is there to say?"

"That I was a damn jealous fool, that's what. I wanted you to be mine, not my father's."

She crossed her arms over her breasts. "I was *not*—"

"Hell, I'm making it worse." He sat up and leaned forward. "I knew he treated you as a daughter. I resented that, too. Because I thought you got more attention from him than I ever did. Mostly, though, I wanted to keep you all to myself. God knows I didn't plan what happened that last night we were together by the moon pool." He rose, crossed to her, sat on the thick white area rug beside the chair and looked up at her. "Give me your hand."

Hesitantly, Maya reached to him and his hand closed around hers, warm and possessive.

"I was wrong to say what I did to you that night," he told her, his gaze as warm as his hand. "Wrong to try to take what you refused to give me willingly. That I was eighteen is some excuse but not much. I knew better, even then."

"What we had was so wonderful." Her voice was barely a whisper as she struggled with conflicting emotions—the agonizing hurt of the past and the equally demanding need of the present. "At sixteen I didn't know much about men and I hated you for ruining the wonder, for changing the beauty to ugliness."

He rose, pulled her from the chair and dropped her hand. He didn't touch her but he stood so close she could feel the heat of his body. "I believe we were meant to come together. Will you let me try to bring back the wonder?" The huskiness in his voice brushed over her like a caress.

How could she resist his plea when she wanted him to hold her so much she ached? He'd said nothing about love but she hadn't expected him to. He'd given her honesty instead, a rare gift, and one she couldn't refuse.

If she was completely honest in return she'd tell him how afraid she was. Not of passion. Not even of loving him. She feared if she said yes, she wouldn't be able to bear the pain when he left Thompsonville, ending what they'd shared. And yet if she said no, she'd have nothing, now and forever.

He smiled faintly. "To paraphrase something I remember from my undergraduate days—the fates lead her who will. Her who won't, they drag. I promise not to drag you but I can't answer for the fates—they're tough cookies."

She laughed and took one step, bringing her up against him. "Who am I to fight fate?" she murmured as his arms closed around her.

All the wonder she'd known at sixteen was there in his kiss, in the lean strength of his body, in the exciting feel of his skin under her fingers. Yet she was no longer a girl. She needed more from him than a boy's kisses and caresses; she wanted everything a man has to give....

Her eager response drove him wild. Never had a woman's mouth tasted as hot and sweet as hers. No woman's skin was so soft and caressable. No woman's scent had ever filled him with such a driving need to possess her. It took all the willpower he possessed to slow down, to savor, to give them both time to learn each other's secrets.

As their kiss deepened, it seemed to him the world shifted, that time slipped out of focus, that the white rug under their feet was the ground beneath the giant sycamores and the soft whirr of the air conditioner the wind whispering among the branches.

His arms tightened around her. She was the center now as she'd been the center then. What did it matter if they were indoors or out? What year it was had no importance. Only she mattered. He buried his hands in the silkiness of her hair, his lips and tongue delighting in the never-forgotten flavor of her skin.

Though urgency pounded through him, his lips lingered at her throat, entranced by her rapid pulse there— proving to him she was as excited as he, as caught up in the sweet and wild communion between them.

His fingers, acting with a will of their own, loosened the ties at her nape and her back so the halter fell away to reveal the beauty of her breasts, to free them for his caress. Her tiny moan of pleasure when he touched her nipple thrilled him, testing his endurance.

He'd waited so long to hold her like this again, and he felt he must be dreaming when she arched to him, offering her breasts for his pleasure and for him to pleasure her.

"Maya." He breathed her name like a prayer.

His mouth on her breasts was almost more than she could bear, yet not enough. A slow, hot spiraling began deep within her, rising, increasing in intensity until she writhed against him, craving more. She clung to him until, both off balance, they eased to the ground.

Or was it the rug? She was no longer certain of where they were. Or of anything other than him. He was her world.

She'd known from that first meeting in the pine grove they were meant to come together. If she hadn't fully understood the implications then, she did now. What was between them was too powerful to be denied. To turn away from what he offered was to turn away from life. She couldn't resist if she wanted to; he infused her with an expanding desire that must be satisfied. By him.

His skin, hot and salty to her tongue, was satin smooth under her fingers, belying the powerful muscles underneath. He'd discarded his tank top and the provocative rasp of his chest hair against her sensitized nipples made her moan.

"Beautiful," he whispered in her ear. "Beautiful Maya."

She wanted to tell him she found him beautiful, too, but his lips covered hers, sealing the words inside. His hand slid up her thigh, stopping at her shorts, and suddenly the barrier of the clothes still between them seemed intolerable. She slipped her hand under the band of his shorts, felt his stomach muscles tense and heard his quick intake of breath.

He helped her and she helped him until all clothes were tossed aside. The hard heat of his body inflamed her and she tried to pull him to her. He resisted, his hands skimming along her curves, touching, caressing, inviting her, leading her to where no man had ever taken her.

Knowing this was meant to be his journey, too, and wanting him with her, she pressed urgently against him.

"Maya?" he asked hoarsely.

"Yes, oh, yes," she murmured.

He eased inside her, slowly at first, then, with a groan, all the way. She cried out, transfixed by the ecstasy of possessing and being possessed. He stopped abruptly and began to withdraw. Caught up in urgent need, she clutched him and rocked her hips, wordlessly demanding more and more. And more.

He began a driving counterpoint to her rhythm and they journeyed together, giving and taking, into a wonder she'd never dreamed existed.

It was some time later when Robert fully realized where he was—stretched out on the rug in the living room of Maya's apartment with Maya in his arms. Filled with a vast contentment, he didn't want to know anything else. Not yet.

"For a while," she said softly, "I didn't know where I was."

"I didn't even know when it was," he admitted, raising himself onto an elbow to look down at her. "Or if I was dreaming." He smoothed a tendril of hair from her forehead. "Have I ever told you how beautiful you are?"

She smiled. "I seem to remember hearing you say something like that."

"I don't think I'm ever going to let you go." He ran a hand over the curve of her hip. "Or stop making love to you."

"I hope not."

He gazed into her amber eyes, refusing to think beyond here and now. She was his, nothing else was important. He considered mentioning that they might shift to her bed but then she lifted her hand and touched his cheek and the light, sweet caress tingled through him, making him forget everything but the need to be inside her, hearing her soft cries of pleasure as they sent each other rocketing.

Much later he woke from a light doze and found her sitting up watching him. "Want to shower first or second?" she asked.

"With," he said.

His beeper went off.

He settled the problem—an order for pain medicine for one of his patients—by talking with the hospital but, when he hung up the phone, he found Maya had taken a quick shower and pulled on a thigh-length T-shirt.

"Your turn," she told him.

As he let the water sluice over him, Robert thought over what had happened. If he'd expected that making love to Maya would solve his need for her, he'd been dead wrong. He already wanted her again. Last night he'd tried to describe to Sal how he felt about her, how the past and the present had run together when they met again and how neither of them could rid themselves of the past unless they came to some decision in the present.

"I won't say I'm in love with her," he'd told Sal. "How the hell do I know what love is? But there's something between us and we both know it's there."

Love was something eighteen-year-olds believed in. He was eleven years past eighteen and there wasn't much he did believe in anymore.

But whatever had been between him and Maya all those years ago sure as hell hadn't been exorcised by what happened today.

She was waiting for him at the table with a glass of orange juice. "You'll pump me so full of vitamin C I'll never get sick again," he teased as he sat down.

"I dreamed about you last night," she told him. "I dreamed you were staked with the grapes in a vineyard."

He set the glass on the table and stared at her, finally shrugging. "If my mother had her way that's where I'd be. Maybe not staked, but committed to the vineyards, tied to Pierson's Pride."

"Your father left Pierson's Pride to you."

"To me and Laura," he corrected. "He knew I'd never live there."

She put her elbows on the table and rested her chin on her hands. "Why?"

"Pierson's Pride was my father's."

"But it was your grandfather's and your great-grandfather's before him. Your father was only a link in a heritage. As you are."

He shook his head. "Not me. Laura, maybe." Discussing his feelings about his father and the vineyard unsettled him so he changed the subject. "Do you know what Sal told me last night? We got to talking about

Laura going off to Stanford and he said he'd always dreamed of someday going to UC Davis.''

"He's never said a word about it to me. But I guess it's not such a surprising dream for an intelligent man."

Robert reached across the table and encircled one of her wrists. "Enough of Sal and everybody except us. I'd like to spend tonight with you."

Maya bit her lip. "I'd like it, too, but no."

Taken aback at her refusal, he released her wrist. "Why not?"

"I'm sort of overwhelmed. I need time to sort things out. Maybe you do, too."

"I need *you.*"

She smiled at him. "Still?"

He rose, pulled her to her feet and drew her against him. She rested her head on his chest and, as he held her, he felt an unaccustomed tenderness. "I thought," he said hesitantly, "I might have hurt you—our first time today, I mean. If I did, I'm sorry. I meant to go slow but if what you do to me could be measured on the Richter scale, it would outclass California's greatest earthquake."

"All the hurting's in the past," she said.

Relieved, he pulled her closer, running his hands down her back to cup her against him. "Hey!" he exclaimed in delight. "You're not wearing anything under that T-shirt...."

When he finally did leave her, it was reluctantly. But as he swung his car from her drive he decided it was just as well she'd refused to let him stay the night. If they shared a bed, neither of them would be in any shape to face the clinic on a manic Monday.

Robert didn't understand how Joe had stood the pressure at the clinic as long as he had without falling apart. No question but that the pace was too much for one doctor to handle. Unfortunately there wasn't enough money to hire a second physician. If only he could figure some way to get the local doctors involved on a *pro bono* basis.

If he practiced in town, he'd be glad to help out a couple of mornings a week, maybe more. San Francisco, though, was too far to commute. Strangely, he wasn't looking forward to returning to his practice there, despite the guaranteed days and weekends off.

He had a feeling Maya wouldn't leave the clinic no matter how he argued about the advantages of her being in San Francisco with him. He'd be leaving her behind. At this point he couldn't make himself believe it would be for the best. Still, after another month, who could tell?

Who're you kidding, Pierson? he asked himself. You'll want her just as badly a month from now. Maybe even more. And you'll be in the city and she'll be here.

So it would be a problem because *he* sure as hell wouldn't stay in Thompsonville, staked to the damn grapevines, like in Maya's dream.

On Monday, Maya opened the back door to go into the clinic with eager anticipation. Though it had been only hours since she'd been with Robert, she could hardly wait to see him again. Never mind that they'd be busy, they'd be together.

She felt she'd been right but she didn't know where she'd found the strength to refuse to allow him to spend the night with her. Deep in her heart she never wanted to be apart from him. Why had she said no?

She thought it might be because she wanted no one to discover what was between her and Robert. It was their secret, not to be shared with anyone. Word got around fast in a small town and the old-timers here had long memories. There'd be those who remembered about Robert's father and her mother. She didn't want them watching and speculating.

She knew better than to think Robert planned to marry her but she didn't want to imagine gossips whispering, "He's a Pierson. He'll never marry her any more than old George married Estella Gabaldon."

Robert was in his office writing up a chart, a cup of coffee on the desk in front of him. He looked up when she stopped in the doorway and his smile made her breath catch.

"Maya. I—"

"Hey," Angela's voice called, "I'm bringing a kid with a rash in—no use spreading whatever he's got to everyone in the waiting room."

And so the Monday rush began early, giving them no time to be alone with each other. But occasionally he'd glance at her over the head of a child he was examining or before ducking into the next room, and for a fleeting moment she'd see the warmth in his eyes that was there for her alone.

Noon brought no respite, lunch was on the run. Near six, as Robert was finishing with the last patient, Angela called to Maya and she hurried into the waiting room, where a dark-haired young woman with frightened eyes stood by Angela's desk. Maya noticed the woman was pregnant.

"Mrs. Luera's husband is sick," Angela said. "She had to leave him in the car."

"In the parking lot?" Maya asked.

Mrs. Luera shook her head. "The car broke down outside town. I walked the rest of the way—wasn't nothing else to do. He's real sick."

"Sick enough for an ambulance?" Maya asked.

Mrs. Luera shook her head. "We ain't got no money. We can't afford the ambulance." Tears shone in her eyes.

"Medi-Cal?" Angela put in.

"Nothing."

"We'll work out something," Maya assured her. "Let me talk to the doctor."

In the end, Robert drove Mrs. Luera to where she'd left the broken-down car, Maya following in her VW. On the shoulder of the highway, under a stand of eucalyptus, Pete Luera, a muscular man in his twenties, sprawled on the back seat of an ancient and battered two-door Ford, his face a mask of pain.

While Maya and Mrs. Luera looked on, Robert pushed forward the front seat and wedged himself partway into the car.

"Pete, I'm Dr. Pierson," he said. "Tell me where it hurts."

"Belly." The word was a groan.

Robert laid his hand on Pete's stomach, pressing gently. "Let me know when I touch the spot that hurts."

Pete groaned in pain when Robert reached the right lower quadrant of his abdomen.

"Acute appendicitis," Maya muttered to herself.

"Pete, we have to get you to a hospital," Robert said. "Okay?"

"Whatever you say, Doc." Pete was obviously in too much pain to take any responsibility for what happened to him.

"Pete's never sick," Mrs. Luera whispered to Maya. "Never."

Maya put an arm around her trembling shoulders. "He'll be all right."

Over Mrs. Luera's feeble protests, Robert called an ambulance. "Don't worry about who'll pay for it," he reassured her. "I'll see the bill's taken care of. And I'll call a tow truck for your car."

"Hey, this guy looks to me like he's got a hot appendix," one of the paramedics said to Robert after they'd loaded Pete into the ambulance. "You sure you want us to take him all the way down to the County Hospital?"

Robert nodded, his face grim. Maya knew what both the paramedic and Robert were thinking—that the appendix might rupture before they reached Bakersfield. I. R. Thompson Hospital was less than a mile away. Pete could be on the operating table in a half hour if he went there. But Robert was an internist, not a surgeon. He didn't have surgical privileges at the hospital and, once the local surgeons discovered the Lueras had no money, who would Robert be able to get to do the appendectomy?

Maya helped Mrs. Luera into the front of the ambulance, pressing five dollars and her phone number into the woman's hand. "If you need a ride back here from Bakersfield, call me," she said.

As the ambulance pulled away, red lights flashing, Robert swore. "No use to admit him to our hospital, even if I could persuade the hospital to take him, when there's not one damn surgeon in town who'd do the appendectomy." Bitterness etched his words. "What's wrong with the heartless bastards?"

"They don't understand," she offered.

"Not from lack of my trying!"

She put a hand on his arm and he pulled her close. "Sometimes," he said, "I think you're the only person who *does* understand."

Chapter Ten

"Do sit down, Robbie," Susan Pierson said, looking up at him from where she sat in her favorite blue-and-gold chair. "Your restlessness makes me nervous. I couldn't bear it when your father paced like that."

Robert stopped, startled. Never in his life did he recall his mother comparing him in any way to his father. He leaned on the marble mantel of the living room fireplace and stared at her, wondering what else of George Pierson she might see in him. He'd always believed he was nothing like this father.

"That's an improvement," she said tartly. "I suppose you're waiting for my comments on what you refer to as the heartlessness of the local physicians. While I sympathize with the problems facing you, I certainly don't think you've been terribly tactful in your approach."

He straightened. "Tactful? What does that have to do with saving a man's life?"

"Tact goes a long way in being persuasive. You have a tendency to rush in and demand."

"But, damn it, I'm right!"

Susan raised her eyebrows. "Being right has very little importance when it comes to getting people to do what you wish. As is apparent when I try to reason with Laura. I absolutely cannot understand your sister's infatuation with a vineyard worker. I expected her to have better taste or at least to show better sense."

"Sal's the overseer, not just an ordinary worker," he reminded her.

Her mouth tightened. "What difference does that make? In any case, I want you to dismiss him immediately."

Robert took a step toward her, unable to believe his ears. "Fire Sal? You can't mean it. Mother, he runs the vineyards. You'd be in trouble without him."

"Mr. Fairfax is the manager. If I'm not mistaken, *he* runs the vineyard. I will not tolerate Salvator Ramirez on the property. If you won't get rid of him, I will."

"You can't." Robert spoke flatly, keeping his anger under tight control. "You can't because I won't agree to any such injustice. Since I'm the legal owner, I have the right to say who goes and who stays. Sal stays."

Her eyes narrowed. "Are you saying you'd put that man's welfare ahead of your sister's?"

"If Sal wanted to take advantage of Laura he's had plenty of chances—she's been throwing herself at him for six months or more. He hasn't and he won't. Laura's the one who needs to be controlled, not Sal."

His mother rose. "Your misplaced loyalty is a direct result of your father's indulgence. When you were a boy, against my wishes he allowed you to trail around after Salvator Ramirez. This is what comes of—of mingling.'' She stalked from the room.

Shaken by the encounter, Robert left the house. Though he hadn't always agreed with his mother, he didn't recall another time when he'd been really angry at her. For much of his life he'd considered himself her protector, the two of them against his father—with Laura, when she came along, too young to be involved.

By the time he was twelve, he'd known, from overhearing gossip, that his father had affairs with other women. Furthermore, he realized his mother was aware of what was going on and that it hurt her deeply. And so it hurt him, too.

Robert shook his head, flung himself into the car and peeled from the driveway. The past, the past, always the past. Why couldn't he get rid of it once and for all?

When he found himself on the road to Maya's, he eased back against the seat, some of the tenseness draining away. At the moment she was exactly what he needed.

''What are you doing here?'' was Maya's greeting, but a warm welcome glowed in her golden eyes. When he wrapped her in his arms, her eager response promised an even warmer welcome to come.

By the time they reached her bedroom, most of his clothes and all of hers were off. Desire simmered in his blood, crackled along his synapses. It was as though he'd never kissed her before, never tasted her sweetness, never felt her supple softness beneath him, as though this were the very first time he'd been so close to her.

He wanted the lovemaking to last forever, meant to make it last as long as he could. If only her breasts weren't so responsive to his touch. If only her abandoned moans didn't drive him to the edge. If only she wasn't flame and fire. If only she wasn't herself then maybe he could hold back and take his time, stretch out the dizzying pleasure for hour after hour.

Once she closed around him, taking him into where he belonged, he lost touch with reality. This was enchantment, bedazzlement; he was enthralled. He'd promised her wonder; instead she gave a wonder to him he hadn't realized existed.

"If you think I'm ever leaving this bed," he said later when his mind finally clicked on again, "you're badly mistaken."

"You agreed we wouldn't meet tonight," she reminded him softly, her breath caressing his ear.

"Temporary insanity. I definitely intend to go on meeting you every night, exactly like this."

"You can't."

He rose up to look at her in the dim light filtering from the hall. "Give me one good reason."

"Dolly Luera is coming to stay with me. I gave her my phone number and once she was sure Pete had survived the surgery and was going to live, she called me. I'm picking her up in Bakersfield before I go to work in the morning."

"Dolly is Pete Luera's wife, I take it."

"Her name's really Dolores. They were on their way from L.A. to Sacramento when his appendix started acting up. He'd heard of the clinic so he turned off the freeway and tried to get to us. Dolly doesn't have a place to stay. Or any money."

"I'll be glad to rent a motel room for her."

"Robert, she's pregnant and she doesn't have anybody but Pete. She's scared and she needs a friend."

Something told him Maya wouldn't go for a suggestion that they might rent a motel room themselves. Actually the idea didn't much appeal to him anyway—he wasn't quite sure why. God knows he wanted her.

He sighed. "This is what I get for taking up with a Good Samaritan."

"As long as we're talking Good Samaritan, aren't you the one who's picking up the tab for the ambulance? And fixing their car?"

"With you taking charge, I have a strong feeling I'll probably wind up finding Pete a job in the vineyard once he recovers."

She hugged him tightly. "Would you?"

He nuzzled her neck. "For another hug like that I might be persuaded to do almost anything."

"Almost?"

"Try me."

"Well, you wanted to take a shower with me yesterday but we didn't have the chance. Actually, I've never taken a shower with anyone before."

Her admission thrilled and aroused him. He got to his feet, pulling her up with him. "Madame, your bath and your bath mate await. It's not the moon pool but it's the best we do at a moment's notice."

She looked at him, her eyes wide and serious. "Oh, but I couldn't bathe with you in the moon pool. Not unless—" She broke off and turned toward the bathroom. "Come on, before your beeper goes off."

He meant to discover why the moon pool was taboo, but once in the shower she very quickly made him forget everything but the feel of her, slick with water, under his hands.

She made popcorn afterward in the kitchen, served with the inevitable orange juice.

"My mother's really upset about Laura's infatuation with Sal," he said. "She asked me to fire him."

Maya paused with her glass halfway to her lips. "Do you let your mother dictate everything you do?"

Slightly taken aback at her question, he said, "You can't seriously believe I'd do such a thing. I'd never fire Sal."

"Wouldn't you? Since you don't care what happens to Pierson's Pride, how can I tell what you might or might not do?"

"Sal's my friend!"

"So you keep saying."

Robert set his glass down with a thunk. "Damn it, are you intimating I'm lying?"

She shook her head. "You believe what you say. You think it's the truth. Yet everyone—even Laura—knows that Sal runs the vineyard, not the incompetent manager your mother hired. Want to try explaining that?"

"How can I? I haven't paid much attention to the place to be able—"

"And why haven't you? Why do you neglect your heritage? Just because you and your father didn't see eye to eye is no excuse to shirk your responsibility to Pierson's Pride."

Anger choked Robert as he tried to respond. How dare she accuse him? Who did she think she was to presume to tell him what to do? She was nothing but a— He stopped abruptly, the direction of his thoughts stunning him. Is that how he truly felt about Maya? That she was a Chicana, nothing but a worker's daughter?

He slumped forward, resting his elbows on the table, his head in his hands, horrified and disgusted at himself.

But I rid myself of prejudice years ago! he argued. Sal's my friend. So's Joe Halago. And now there's Maya.

Eleven years ago there'd been Maya, too. What had he told himself all those years ago, once he'd learned who she was? *That she was a Gabaldon-Najero and, because of her ancestry and background, not worthy of a Pierson. Not worthy of him.*

"Oh my God," he muttered, wondering if deep inside he still felt that way.

Impossible! That would make him a world-class creep.

"Robert?" Maya sounded concerned.

He couldn't talk to her now, couldn't explain. "I have to go," he mumbled, rising, stumbling to the door, hardly aware of what he was doing.

All he knew was he had to get away, had to be alone.

The next morning, on the drive back from Bakersfield, Maya did her best to discover if the Lueras had any relatives in L.A., where their journey had begun. She hoped to find someone who could help them.

At first Dolly just kept shaking her head but finally she sighed. "I got to talk to somebody," she said. "Pete and me, we can't go back to L.A. A month ago Pete's boss lost his business. Everybody working for him was out of a job and the men didn't even get paid for the last two weeks they worked. I had a job as a nurse's assistant but Pete didn't like me working on account of the baby so I quit just before this happened—so all of a sudden we didn't have no money."

Dolly bit her lip. "We couldn't pay the rent and so we had to get out of our apartment. We went to stay with his cousin Manny—that's our only relative in this country. Manny's wife, she left him a couple of months ago and he was pretty broke up and all and drinking too much on account of it. He smoked a lot, even in bed. That used to scare me but what could I say—it was his place, not mine. Anyway, this one night when Manny'd been drinking, somehow he set the place on fire. We slept in the living room so we got out okay but nothing was left of our stuff, and poor Manny, he died."

"How terrible!" Maya exclaimed.

"Yeah, it was awful, all right. Pete took it extra hard 'cause he tried to get in the bedroom to save Manny but the flames were too bad. Even the firemen couldn't do it. They told us likely Manny died of smoke inhalation so he didn't feel pain but that didn't make Pete feel no better."

"It sounds as though no one could have saved Manny."

"I know that and I guess Pete does but he's been real down about it—can't get Manny off his mind. At the funeral we heard about work at some ranch by Sacramento with a place to stay so we decided to drive up there. Pete, he wanted to get out of L.A. I didn't blame him. Besides, I thought leaving there'd help him stop thinking about how Manny died and all that. Only we never got to Sacramento. We never got any further than here."

Maya tried for a reassuring smile. "If you want to, maybe we can find a way for you and Pete to stay here, at least until he gets on his feet again."

"You've done a lot already. We can't begin to pay you back."

"Don't be too sure. La Raza Clínica could use a volunteer nurse's assistant for a few hours a day—if you feel up to it. You could keep busy until Pete's released from the hospital and it would help the clinic at the same time. That's paying me back and Dr. Pierson, too.''

''I'll do it! Nothing's wrong with me—the baby don't give me no problems.''

''You can start tomorrow. You've been up all night worrying over Pete. You and that baby need to rest today.''

Maya took Dolly home, showed her where everything was and drove to work. The Lueras' troubles had temporarily taken her mind off Robert's odd departure last night but, as she neared the clinic, she puzzled over what had caused him to leave so abruptly.

Though she was sure it had something to do with the way she'd confronted him about neglecting Pierson's Pride, she was still confused. First he'd gotten angry— that, she could understand—but then he'd behaved almost like someone who'd been hit over the head. Nothing she'd said could have had that much impact!

As she pulled into the parking lot, Robert was just opening the back door to go inside. He didn't see her. When she was a child and caught a glimpse of him, she used to be reminded of the golden-haired princes in the fairy-tale books at school. Prince Robert of Pierson's Pride.

He still carried himself with the unconscious arrogance of a man born to rule. Arrogant or not, her heart lifted at the sight of him.

She parked and went in, pausing as she passed his office, but he wasn't at his desk. He was leafing through a file cabinet with his back to her. She waited a moment but he didn't turn so she walked on, feeling both deflated and miffed. He must have heard the back door open; he must have known she'd come in. What in those files was so important he couldn't have flashed her a quick smile? If something was wrong, why not say so?

Put a hold on the personal, she ordered herself. You're at work so be professional.

Maya took a deep breath, stowed her bag and began checking the rooms to make certain they were in order for patients to be seen.

As the morning went on, Robert talked to her—but only about the medical problems they were treating. Mrs. Guerrera, a tiny, wrinkled woman of eighty-eight with heart trouble, was the last patient before lunch.

"You're eighty-eight percent better," Robert told her when he finished listening to her chest.

Mrs. Guerrera smiled. "You want to know why, Doctor?"

"Could be you've finally decided to take your medicine regularly," he said.

The old woman pointed at Maya. "*La Curandera,* she tell me those pills you give me come from plant that grows to help sick hearts. Me, I know plant medicine is good, so now I take those pills. Every day. You lucky you got *La Curandera* to help. She make sick people get well."

"I guess I am," he told her.

Mrs. Guerrera shook her head. "No guess. You lucky."

Robert glanced at Maya as the old woman left the room but she couldn't read his expression. Was he angry? Amused? She certainly had no intention of apologizing for being called *La Curandera* by her people.

"Starting tomorrow, Dolly Luera will be working here a few hours a day as a nurse's assistant volunteer," she told him, since she could think of nothing else to say.

"You're good at organizing people's lives, aren't you?" he said.

Maya felt his remark was no compliment but a reaction to what she'd said last night about his lack of interest in Pierson's Pride. Ignoring that, she bit back a sharp retort and finished what she'd meant to say. "Pete worked for a landscaper in Los Angeles. He might prove useful in the vineyard."

Robert nodded. Absently, she thought. As though his mind weren't on Pete. Or Dolly. Or her. Concealing her disappointment at his lack of interest, she marched past him into the hall. When would she learn that Robert Pierson wasn't to be trusted?

Robert left the clinic before six, avoiding any possibility of being left alone with Maya. He'd seldom felt less like working; he'd thought the day would never end.

What the hell was the matter with him? A week ago he'd have found Mrs. Guerrera's words amusing. Today they'd fallen like stones on his heart. The old woman had told the truth as she saw it and, damn it, he had to admit he agreed with her. Maya had a gift; she was a natural healer.

His healing came from books, hers from some intuitive center within her. She instinctively knew things he'd never learned and he found it unsettling. He smiled wryly. The old gal was right—it did make them a good team.

He was a lucky man. He parked his Italian coupe in the doctor's space at the hospital but didn't get out. Lucky. Yeah, real lucky.

Lucky to have lied to himself all his life?

What if he'd spewed forth all those biased words last night? Called Maya a Chicana. Called her nothing but a worker's daughter. Like his prejudiced mother might do.

Maya would have thrown him out of her apartment. Out of her life. Everything between them would be over. The wonder lost, defiled.

He closed his eyes, his hands gripping the wheel. He'd always been so sure he was right. Sure of what he was, who he was, how he thought. Somehow all of that had been erased. He was no longer certain of anything.

He didn't want to go into the hospital. He didn't really need to see his inpatients again today—they were all doing well. He didn't want to go home. He didn't think he could bear talking to his mother at the moment. Where else was there? He couldn't even find a bar and get drunk because there was no doctor to cover for him in case of an emergency. Nowhere to go. No one to talk to.

Even if Maya hadn't invited the Luera woman to stay with her, he couldn't go there. Not until he came to terms with what he was. Who'd want him in this state? He sure didn't care for his own company.

After a time he raised his head, nodded and started the car. He did have one possibility.

He found Sal standing in the shade of a giant mulberry, grooming Padrino. About to call, *"Hola, compadre,"* Robert found the words sticking in his throat, unsure if they were patronizing. He walked toward Sal in silence and stood watching him curry the horse.

"Just a friendly visit or you got a reason?" Sal asked at last.

"I don't know."

Sal turned from Padrino to stare at him. "What's wrong?"

Robert shrugged. Now that he was here, he didn't know what to say.

"Rob, I'm no good at guessing—anything I can do, tell me."

Robert struggled to find words but none came to him. Finally, since he could think of nothing else, he said, "This couple, Luera's their name, need a place to live. He's in the County Hospital, just had an appendectomy, and Maya took in his wife temporarily. Do you know of anything for rent?"

"Not offhand. But I've got room—they could stay with me until they find something."

"I didn't mean you should take them in."

Sal waved a hand. "No big deal." He grinned. "If the lady can cook a halfway decent meal, I may even come out ahead."

Robert couldn't help thinking how his mother would react if he brought the Lueras to Pierson's Pride to stay for a few days. Never mind how big the house was— she'd never willingly take in a Chicano family. Or any poor family, he supposed. She hadn't been brought up to extend charity to those in need—not on a personal level. You might give money to charity but you didn't invite people who weren't "your kind" into your house and that was that.

Yet Maya and Sal, both with far less than the Piersons, had offered to share what they had with stranded strangers.

How about me? Robert wondered. If it were my San Francisco condo, would I take in the Lueras?

True, he meant to cover the cost of the ambulance and fixing their car, but since he could well afford to, how personal was that? Wasn't it about the same as his mother donating money to charities?

"Thanks, Sal," he said. "Another thing—I may want to offer Pete Luera a job in the vineyards. Apparently he worked for a landscaper. See what you think about his possibilities."

Sal raised his eyebrows but all he said was "Sure. Anything else?"

"I guess that's it." Reluctantly, Robert prepared to leave.

"I'm going riding in a half hour or so," Sal said. "In the hills, just to give Padrino some exercise. Want to join me? If you haven't forgotten how, we could bring ropes and try some fancy láriat tossing."

Like old times, he and Sal riding together and fooling around with roping tricks. There was nothing he'd rather do right now. "Emperor could stand a run," he said. "Where'll we meet?"

"How about that stand of eucalyptus where Culpepper Road cuts across Pierson property?"

"I'll be there." Belatedly recalling a forbidden pleasure from their rides in the old days, Robert added, "And I'll bring the beer."

"Good, 'cause I'm fresh out."

By the time Robert rode up to the trees by Culpepper Road, Sal was waiting.

"Hola, compadre!" Sal called.

When he heard the familiar words, a surge of relieved pleasure all but overwhelmed Robert. No matter what he'd done or hadn't done, no matter what his failings, Sal was his companion. His friend.

He reined in when he reached the trees, grabbed a can of cold beer from his saddlebag, tossed it to Sal and waited for what he knew would come.

Sal popped the tab and took a long swallow. Speaking in Spanish, he quoted an old Mexican proverb. "Now I'm like a fish in water."

Robert grinned as he gave the expected tag line. "Wet and happy!"

He realized as they rode into the hills that he didn't have to try to talk to Sal about his problems. Being with him, like in the old days, was enough.

On Wednesday evening, as Maya and Dolly were washing the supper dishes, the phone rang.

"Sal!" Maya said, recognizing his voice. "Robert told me Dolly and Pete will be staying with you. That's great. You're one in a million."

"It'll work out," he said. "What's wrong between you and Rob?"

She took a deep breath. "What makes you think anything is?"

"When he acts like a downed hawk, something's wrong and I figured it had to be with you."

"You also should have figured it's none of your business."

"Come on, cuz, don't feed me that. I'm your friend, I'm his friend."

"Good. We both need friends. Especially the kind who can take a hint."

Sal sighed. "Okay, I'll keep out of it."

They discussed when Pete would be released from the hospital and who'd pick him up. Finally Sal said, "A note from Laura came in the mail—a lot of stuff about true hearts never being apart. No real sense to it but I figure she must be planning something *loco* again. Maybe you better talk to her before she drops the bunch of us in the manure pile one more time."

"Have you seen her since that night she rode to your house?"

"Not once. I was hoping it'd stay that way until she left for Stanford. But she's like a grasshopper. If she can't leap, she'll fly. You can't keep her down." Annoyed admiration tinged his words.

"I'll try to talk to her," Maya promised, "but don't expect miracles."

"The sooner you do it the better. Tonight, if possible. And don't use the phone. They've got too many extensions in there."

The last place Maya wanted to go was to the Pierson house. If it was for anyone but Sal, she wouldn't. She wanted to help him. And help Laura, too, if she could. She was far from certain anything she could say would stop the girl from whatever she might be planning, but she'd do her best.

As she changed from cutoffs and a halter to a bright yellow sleeveless cotton dress, she wondered exactly who she was putting on one of her newest outfits for. Mrs. Pierson? Laura? Or Robert, on the off chance she'd see him?

What was wrong with him? she asked herself as she ran a brush through her hair. If it's over between us, can't he say so instead of behaving so politely at work that it sets my teeth on edge?

And why was it over? Because he didn't want her anymore? Because he was angry over what she'd said? Why? Her lips tightened. If she grew any more miserable, she might just ask him.

"I'll be back in an hour," she told Dolly as she picked up her keys.

Driving to Pierson's Pride, Maya rehearsed possible scenarios. In the one most likely, Susan would refuse to let her talk to Laura. What then? She could hardly force her way into the house. If she was lucky, Laura would be around when she rang the bell and they could bypass Susan.

If that happened, what was she to say to the girl to convince her Sal was best left alone?

How about *I've come to advise you that love can only break your heart. I should know because I was foolish enough to let your brother break mine. Twice.*

Chapter Eleven

At first Maya thought she was in luck because Robert's coupe wasn't in the driveway—one less Pierson she'd have to encounter. But then Susan opened the door and stood staring at her. Or maybe glaring was more accurate.

Though it appeared Susan wasn't likely to let her in the house, much less allow her to talk to her daughter, Maya gathered her courage and said, "Good evening, Mrs. Pierson. I'd like to see Laura."

After a long, tension-filled moment, Susan stepped back, "We'd better discuss this inside."

Wondering why seeing Laura was a matter for discussion, Maya entered warily and followed Susan into a small room off the entry, full of plants and furnished with white wicker. Since she was not invited to sit down, she didn't. Neither did Susan.

"Apparently you're not a part of this scheme," Susan said. She thrust a piece of paper at Maya.

Glancing at the note, Maya recognized Laura's childish scrawl.

Mom: I've gone to Sal. I know you won't be happy about it, but Sal and I do love each other. Please try to forgive me. By the time you read this we'll be on our way to be married.

Shocked, Maya handed the paper back to Susan. "I don't understand—" she began.

"*You* don't understand!" Susan's voice rose. "What about me? An elopement! How could she do this? How could she?"

"Mrs. Pierson, I don't believe Sal would—"

Susan didn't seem to hear her. "Running off with Salvator Ramirez, of all men. Eloping is foolish enough but why did she have to choose him? It was his idea, of course. He's the devious type. He planned this very carefully. Older men who take advantage of innocent young girls are despicable. And any man who'd use a naive girl like Laura to advance his position in life is lower than the lowest."

Susan twisted the note in her fingers. "Why does no one listen to me? I warned Robbie what would happen. I told him to get rid of Mr. Ramirez once and for all— but did he agree? No, he had the nerve to defend the man, if you can imagine!"

When Susan paused to take a breath, Maya tried to cut in. "I think you should know that Sal is my—"

"It's too bad Laura's father isn't alive to horsewhip Salvator Ramirez—whipping's what he deserves." Susan clenched her fists, crumpling the note.

Maya had tried to keep a leash on her rising anger but Susan's last words were too much for her. "George Pierson would never have horsewhipped anyone! If you were one-hundredth as understanding and fair-minded as George was you'd realize my cousin Sal is an honorable man. It's a shame Laura is stirring up this mess because she has a crush on Sal but he'd never take advantage of an infatuated teenager. Never."

Susan drew herself up. "Are you presuming to tell me what my own husband was like? And speaking of taking advantage—that's exactly what you did. You took advantage of George's foolish weakness for your mother to forward your own self-interest. I know you wheedled money from him. Never think I don't. Money that rightly should have gone to his own children."

Maya, blinking back tears of mixed hurt and fury, took a deep breath. She wouldn't give Susan the satisfaction of seeing her cry.

"Yes," she said, "George paid for my education as a nurse. It was a generous gift he gave me—the chance to help my people. But the greatest gift he gave me wasn't money. It was the affection of a father."

Maya knew she should shut up and leave but she couldn't stop the words from pouring out. "No one is perfect. I'm not claiming George was but I do know he helped others besides me. Instead of blaming your husband for his faults, why not appreciate the good he did?"

That's enough, a voice in her head warned. Leave!

Turning on her heel, Maya marched to the door. Before she touched the knob, the door flew open and Laura rushed inside. She stopped when she saw Maya and her mother, her gaze shifting from one to the other. Her face puckered like a child's and she burst into tears.

"Sal doesn't love me!" Laura wailed. "He hates me!"

"He doesn't hate you." Maya pitched her voice low and soothing.

"But he *does* hate me. If he didn't, he wouldn't have dumped me in my car like a—a sack of fertilizer and driven me right back home."

Maya laid a gentle hand on her shoulder. "Look, Laura, Sal's a lot older than you. Maybe not old enough to be your father but almost. I've told you that your own father and I were friends—George Pierson was a substitute for my father, who died before I was born.

"I'm sure George was a good father to you and it's your bad luck he didn't live to give you the affection you craved. You were like me—you needed a father and you substituted Sal. But you mistook your feeling for him and tried to find a different kind of love, a love he couldn't give you. But that doesn't matter. Sal will understand and still be your friend. He'll always be your friend, just as George was always mine."

Laura stared at her, tears running down her cheeks. "But I don't want a friend!" she wailed, and fled toward the stairs. Susan started after her.

Maya left the house and hurried toward her car. An increasingly uncomfortable suspicion that she'd said far too much to Susan, combined with mixed exasperation and concern for Laura, made her eager to drive off and never come near the place again.

She stopped abruptly when she saw the Italian sports car parked next to Laura's convertible and her own VW. Robert had come home. Glancing around, she didn't see him, so she slid into her car, hoping to leave before he materialized. But as she turned the key in the ignition, he strode into the beams of her headlights.

He put his hands on the frame of her open window and leaned down. "Where are you going?"

"Home."

"Wait." He walked behind the VW and called, "Take my car, Sal. I left the keys in it." Then, before she realized what he intended, he slid into her passenger seat. "Now we're ready to go home," he said.

"You are home," she pointed out.

"I prefer yours at the moment. My mother and Laura need time to calm down before I set foot in the door."

"Dolly's at my place," she reminded him.

"Not for long. Pete was released from the County Hospital late this afternoon. Instead of calling anyone, he got a ride to Thompsonville with an off-duty paramedic who drove him to the hospital here because Pete didn't know where else to go. The hospital notified me, I picked him up and was on my way to Sal's with him when Sal passed me, driving Laura's car. I dropped Pete off and came home to see what the hell was going on. I found Sal ready to hike home and he filled me in on Laura's latest brainstorm."

"She's devastated."

"So is he. There seems to be a generally devastating fallout from all of Laura's escapades. I'm going to do my damnedest to make sure this is her last. Now let's hit the road. We've got to play more musical cars before the night's over."

They drove in silence to Maya's, where they picked up Dolly and brought her to Sal's in the VW. There Robert changed to his own car and Maya both hoped and feared that Robert wouldn't follow her to her apartment.

When he turned off toward town, she sighed, not sure how much was from relief and how much from disappointment. Aware she was too unsettled to sleep, she put off going to bed, opting for TV, only to find that nothing interested her. She'd just shut it off when the doorbell rang.

She opened the door slightly, leaving the chain on. Robert stood on her doorstep with a boxed pizza in one hand and a paper bag in the other.

"Won't you join me?" he asked, entering when she unhooked the chain.

"I've already eaten."

"I haven't and I hate to eat alone. Sit down with me and pretend you're hungry."

The bag contained two chocolate shakes. "I've OD'd on OJ," he told her, placing a shake on each side of the table. "Living in an orange grove provides too much of a good thing."

Seeing the pizza had anchovies, she couldn't resist trying a slice. And she couldn't deny she loved chocolate, no matter what form it came in.

"I shouldn't be here," he said as he finished the last crumb.

"You weren't invited," she pointed out.

"Yeah, I know I've been impossible."

Surprised that he'd admit it made her smile. "Impossible but polite about it," she agreed.

"Sal and I went riding in the hills earlier this evening. That helped."

Helped what? she wanted to ask but didn't.

"I'm not ready to talk about it," he added as though she had asked. "I can't." He rose from the table, came around to where she sat, lifted her from the chair and pulled her into his arms. "You don't know how many times I've wanted to hold you."

He smelled faintly of horse and of male sweat, odors she'd never before found irresistible. She did now. She wanted nothing more than to stay where she was—permanently. Resistance took a tremendous effort but she forced herself to step back.

"I won't be treated like a disposable glove," she told him.

Robert looked startled for a moment, then chuckled. He was still smiling when he cupped her face in his hands but the smile gradually faded as he looked intently into her eyes.

"I'd never throw you away," he murmured. "Never. What happened to me was my fault, not yours. I still haven't straightened things out in my own mind but if I try to stay away from you until I do, I'll go *muy mucho loco.* Very much crazy."

His eyes promised her more than his words. Still, if she gave in to her urge to melt into his embrace, she'd be back where she started. What it came down to was should she make herself miserable now or opt for the misery she feared would come later, when he left Thompsonville?

His lips covered hers, the kiss a thrilling prelude to what was to follow. How could she turn away from the coruscating magic between them?

She thought of a Mexican proverb her grandfather loved to quote. *Time is gold.* Her time with Robert was precious. Deciding she'd enjoy the days she could have with him, she surrendered to his embrace.

After long delicious moments he lifted his head. "How are the mosquitoes around here?" he asked.

She blinked in confusion. "I haven't been bothered."

"Good. Because I want to make love to you outdoors."

On the hill, she thought instantly, excited by the idea of being with him under the stars.

Robert carried an old quilt over his shoulder as they walked through the grove, each with an arm around the other, stopping often to kiss.

"Much more of this and we'll never get to the hill," he told her. "We'll wind up under the orange trees with all the wriggling little nematodes."

She laughed. "What a romantic picture you paint, Doctor."

"That's not what my English comp prof used to write on my essays. I remember one time she was reduced to commenting that at least I could spell."

When they finally reached the top, he spread the quilt on the dry summer grass before pulling her down to sit beside him. The warm night breeze carried the sweetness of gardenias from someone's garden and a hint of the grapes ripening in the nearby fields. The not-quite-half moon, low in the western sky, cast little light, but they had no need of anything brighter than starshine.

Somewhere in the orange grove below a mockingbird burst into song, showering the night with its music, while high overhead, jets, probably from the nearby air force base, provided a faint and distant background thrumming.

"What are you thinking about?" he asked as he stretched out and drew her down beside him.

"You," she answered truthfully. When wasn't he in her thoughts?

"Did you ever think about me in those eleven years we were apart?"

"Not if I could help it. And not favorably."

"I banned you entirely," Robert said, "but sometimes you slipped into my dreams. There's a song about a white dove that flies to freedom. I never knew why that song haunted me until I met you again. In my dreams you always disappeared like an escaping dove, leaving me behind."

Remembering what she'd dreamed about the two of them on this very hill, Maya bit her lip. It would be too revealing, too much an exposure of her fears, to confess how her dream foreshadowed their separation.

"Don't disappear, Maya." He whispered the words into her ear, his warm breath a caress.

"No," she murmured, knowing she wouldn't be the one who flew away.

She turned her head, seeking and finding his lips, relishing the spicy taste of his mouth and the excitement of his tongue tasting her. Her body, anticipating fulfillment, was eager for him but she wanted to draw out the expectation, to savor the tang of each kiss and the pleasure of each caress as her need and his mounted to a dizzying, urgent wildness.

Each time with him was unique, a new and fascinating experience enticing her to offer more, to take more.

She slid her hands under his shirt and absorbed the heat and texture of his skin through her palms and fingertips. If only she could spend the rest of her life touching him and being touched by him.

"I think of you as an outdoor creature," he murmured huskily. "Not quite tamed, always poised to flee."

"Not from you." She heard her passion roughening her voice.

"Not from me," he echoed. "Stay with me, Maya, my Maya."

His words fell on her heart.

Urgency overwhelmed her. Consumed by desire, she burned for him, all of him. Clothes disappeared, lips and fingers caressed, hands sought and found.

When at last they joined together, the world fell away and left the two of them suspended in the wonder they'd created.

Sometime later she lay looking up at the sky with her head pillowed on his stomach, his fingers idly winding strands of her hair into curls.

"The moon has set," she said.

"That sounds like the beginning of one of those poems in English lit that I could never relate to," he told her.

"A one-track science mind?"

"I didn't think anything was wrong with that at the time."

"But now?"

He tugged gently on a strand of her hair. "It's all your fault. You've made me take another look at myself."

She waited but he didn't say anything more. "And have you found a poet hidden deep inside you?" she asked finally.

"Who knows? I'm not down that far yet. I'm still trying to come to terms with how you healed Laura."

"Too bad I couldn't cure her of her infatuation for Sal."

He sighed. "I hate to go home to the turmoil her one-sided elopement has stirred up."

"Poor Laura. Growing up is tough."

He swung her around until she half lay on top of him. "We ought to know, right? Thank God we finally made it." He ran a hand down her back and over the curve of her hip. "You feel so good to touch. I may never stop."

Warm tingles chased one another through her body, making her believe that if she was a cat she'd be purring. Catlike, she touched her tongue to his chest to taste his salt flavor.

"No, damn it, not English lit," he said suddenly. "What I remember comes from that one drama course I suffered through—ancient Greek plays and all that. The prof had a thing about Sappho. He was always pacing about the room spouting her lines. Here's the quote I was reminded of. 'The moon has set, and the Pleiades; it is midnight, and time passes, and I sleep alone.'"

Maya shivered.

"Are you cold?" His voice was concerned.

She shook her head. She might be naked but the chill was inner, not outer. It was after midnight and she wasn't alone; he was with her. But what of all the midnights to come?

"I'm not up on my constellations," she said to mask her unhappy presentiment. "Where are the Pleiades?"

"They're in Taurus the bull—the seven stars that form his neck."

"One astronomy course, too?" she asked lightly.

"You got it. I was as single-minded as premeds come. I barely tolerated the university's efforts to broaden my scope. I'm still single-minded when it comes to what I want." As he spoke, he eased her completely on top of him.

Desire quickened her breathing—in this position there was no mistaking his meaning.

"The problem," he whispered into her ear, "is to convince you."

She traced his upper lip with the tip of her tongue, pausing before she started on the lower to murmur, "What problem?"

"I see I was mistaken," he said as he raised her hips to settle her onto him. "The lady *is* for burning."

He groaned as she took him into her. There were no more words, no need for words, as they began their passionate rhythm.

Much later he said, "I don't even want to know what time it is."

Neither did she but, unfortunately, the glowing hands of his watch were only inches from her eyes. "Ten after one," she informed him.

He got to his feet. "I wish I didn't have to leave you but sooner or later I have to go home and listen to my mother tell me how distraught she is over Laura's behavior. She'll also ask for advice and then not take it. Since it's typical of her to wait up for me when she's upset, I might as well get it over with."

Best to be fair, even to the enemy, Maya told herself as she rose and pulled on her clothes. "Your mother has a right to be upset. Laura acted very selfishly."

"I thought you'd take Laura's side."

"I *am* on her side. I'm sure she's more miserable than anyone else, but that's no excuse to behave like a two-year-old."

"Personally, I feel sorry for Sal." Robert folded the quilt, slung it over one shoulder and grasped Maya's hand. "Imagine how the poor guy felt to come home to the scene Laura arranged. He knew she was there because he saw the convertible but he had no idea she'd stolen a key to his house. He found her draped across his bed in a see-through shortie nightgown."

"Oh, no!"

"Take it from me, that's not easy on any guy."

Maya thought of what Laura had told her about getting Sal to go to bed with her and shook her head, not certain whether she pitied Sal or Laura the most. "Why does love cause so many problems?"

Robert snorted. "She's not in love."

"Whatever you want to call it, remember it feels like love to Laura. No wonder she felt so humiliated. Sal rejected her as a woman."

"He rejected her because she *isn't* a woman."

"Not from Laura's point of view. She offered herself, he turned her down. It might be the first time anyone's ever rejected her. Don't be too hard on her. She's suffering. It's always a shock to discover you can't have everything you want—or even the one thing you want most in the world. Many of us learn the lesson at a much younger age. Like about two."

Robert squeezed her hand. "*I* was eighteen."

She smiled at him in the darkness of the grove, moved by his confession.

"Like Laura," he said. "I brought it on myself by being selfish."

"You should have tried a little tenderness," she said wryly.

He leaned over and brushed her lips with his. "Yeah, *now* you tell me."

They'd almost reached the house when he said, "Laura's tough enough to survive. My mother's the real problem."

In more ways than one, Maya thought. Aloud, she said, "Your mother blames Sal."

"I figured as much. She's always closed her eyes to Laura's devious little ways. She'll probably refuse to believe a word I say."

"You're very fond of your mother." It wasn't a question. He deferred to Susan constantly, treating her as though she were fragile and likely to break into pieces if he dared disagree with her. Personally, she thought Susan had an iron will that no one and nothing could ever shatter.

"She and I have always been close. My father—" He paused and didn't go on.

It was time the words were said. "Your father loved my mother and she loved him—to the day they died."

They'd come into the circle of light cast by the lamp near the drive so she saw Robert's nod.

"My mother knew." His voice was tinged with sadness. "She never got over it."

Maya pulled her hand from his, stopped and faced him. "Why not? My mother died so young. She was gone long before Laura was born. What had your mother to fear from a dead woman?"

Robert shifted his shoulders. "There were other women."

Maya bit her lip. Before she left Thompsonville she'd heard the rumors about George but had refused to believe them—because she didn't want to. Now she suspected they were true. George had been a man who loved life in all its aspects. If his marriage was unhappy...

"That's too bad," she said.

"Theirs was a rotten marriage. I know she was in love with him, despite everything, but I've often wondered why he married her."

"Because Estella Gabaldon was the daughter of a Chicano vineyard worker and Piersons don't marry beneath them." She noted the bitterness in her words but felt she had the right to resentment.

Robert stared at her. "If he really wanted her, that shouldn't have stopped him."

The same thing her grandfather had told her. "I loved your father," she said slowly. "I knew him well enough

to understand he wasn't a fighter. He was a born concil-
iator, a peacemaker.''

Robert grimaced. ''Maybe. All I know is he made my
mother miserable. Seeing her suffer turned me off marriage completely.'' He shrugged. ''I've seen nothing since
to change my mind.''

His words hit her like a blow—never mind that she'd
been aware all along that he wouldn't marry *her*. This,
though, was a clear announcement that he didn't plan to
marry anyone.

Instead of making her feel better, she felt worse.

Okay, so he'd made his declaration of independence.
So what? She raised her chin.

''You'd better run along home,'' she said coolly.
''Especially if your mother's waiting up for you.''

He grasped her shoulders. ''No. Don't do that. Don't
turn cold. If something's wrong, tell me.''

''What could possibly be wrong?''

He scowled. ''How should I know? But it's obvious
something is. I won't leave you like this.''

She jerked free. ''You encase yourself in a block of ice
for days and you expect me to understand that you're
struggling with personal problems you can't share with
anyone.'' Her voice rose. ''Did it ever occur to you that
I might have a problem or two that I don't care to share
with you?''

He gripped her arms, pulling her close to him. ''We're
damn well going to share something.'' His mouth came
down on hers angrily, without tenderness, demanding a
response.

She stiffened momentarily but her own hunger betrayed her, softening her so she melted against him, her
lips parting beneath his.

His kiss gentled, persuading rather than forcing. His hands molded her to him, making his arousal obvious to her.

"Now see what you've done," he said against her lips.

"Sure, blame me."

"Who else?" He kissed her again, hard and deep and urgent. When he broke from the kiss he didn't release her but buried his face in her neck. "Maya," he whispered. "Maya, Maya."

Thrilled by his desire, weak with her need for him, she held him to her, willing herself not to say the three forbidden words trembling on her tongue. The fact that she loved him was the only thing she could hold back, the one part of her she'd never give him.

Chapter Twelve

Robert had planned to slip in through the side door, but when he saw the light on in the living room, he sighed and gave up. As he'd thought, his mother was awake and waiting for him. Fond as he was of his mother, it was a habit of hers he'd never appreciated, not as a teenager and certainly not as an adult.

"There you are," she said when he entered the room. Unsaid but implicit was the "finally." Her glance raked him up and down, taking in his boots, jeans and rumpled T-shirt. "You should know better than to show up at the hospital dressed like that."

He said nothing, understanding she suspected he hadn't been at the hospital. He wasn't eighteen, like Laura, so his private life was none of his mother's business and he didn't intend to get into any discussion of what he'd been doing.

"Well," she said, "I hope you're satisfied. I warned you to dismiss that Ramirez man. You didn't see fit to listen to me and look what happened. What do you intend to do about him now?"

Robert took a deep breath, aware he had to be firm and hoping he had the energy. "It's late, I'm tired and I have a busy day tomorrow. I can't even think, much less talk coherently. I'm putting this discussion on hold until after I'm through at the clinic tomorrow." He kept his gaze focused on her. "To be fair, neither of us will make a decision of any kind until we've had a talk."

Susan sniffed. "Postponement solves no problems, but if you refuse to discuss the matter until tomorrow I suppose I have no choice but to wait."

He smiled at her, relieved that she'd capitulated without an argument. "No choice," he agreed. Crossing to where she sat on the couch, he kissed her cheek. "Good night, Mother."

When the alarm buzzed at seven, he struggled up from the dark well of sleep and got himself ready to make hospital rounds before going to the clinic.

He couldn't decide which he enjoyed the most—reaching the clinic before Maya and anticipating her arrival or arriving later and knowing she'd be there when he came in. Either way, the first sight of her every morning made his heart lift. No other woman had ever moved him the way she did. The proud sweep of her high cheekbones, her glowing amber eyes set slightly aslant, her full, enticing lips and the graceful curves of her body—just thinking about her was enough to arouse him.

Though the wide variety of ailments he diagnosed and treated at the clinic kept him involved, his work was spiced by having her beside him. He didn't relish the thought of leaving Thompsonville. Returning to his city practice would be a tremendous letdown in more ways than one....

The day went well until Sal called him at noon.

"Sorry to bother you at the clinic," Sal said, "but we've got a problem in the vineyards. I know Pete can't start work for another week but he asked me to bring him with me this morning so he could take a look around. I figured no harm to that, so I did."

"Is Pete all right?"

"Pete's okay. The problem's Fairfax. He ordered Pete off the property."

Robert frowned. "Why?"

"He claims Pete's not an employee. I told him you might be hiring Pete and he blew. Said *he* was the only person who hired and fired and if I didn't like it I could leave. I kept my mouth shut, took off with Pete and came home for lunch, but I want you to know I sure as hell don't feel like going back. Ever."

"Hang in there. I'll be over as soon as I see one more patient."

Robert found Sal sitting on the porch of his cottage, scowling. Sal gave him no greeting.

"Hot out here," Robert observed.

"Yeah." Anger simmered in Sal's voice. "Like me right now. Hell, I wasn't claiming to be in charge. I know better. The man was tossing accusations like a damn baler gone haywire."

"Look, take some time to cool off, okay? At least wait until I talk to Fairfax before you do anything rash."

Not meeting Robert's gaze, Sal leaned over the porch rail and spat onto the ground.

"I don't blame you for being disgusted," Robert said. "It's no wonder you're ready to give up on everything to do with Piersons—first Laura's escapades and now Fairfax dumping on you. No call for either. But Pierson's Pride needs you, Sal. *I* need you there.''

Sal's sidelong glance was opaque—Robert couldn't read the expression in his eyes. ''Okay,'' he said finally. ''I'll wait till you talk to Fairfax. But I don't promise anything else.''

Robert had never exchanged more than a word or two with Vince Fairfax, a brown-haired man in his mid-thirties, impeccably dressed today in a tan shirt and matching tan chinos, clean and unwrinkled. Even his boots held a shine. No vineyard manager who worked at his job ever looked that neat.

''I understand you've had a misunderstanding with the foreman,'' Robert began.

''Mr. Ramirez seems to feel he's running the place,'' Fairfax replied. ''I set him straight.''

According to both Laura and Maya, that's exactly what Sal *had* been doing—running the place while Fairfax sat back and let him. From what Robert had observed, they weren't far off the mark. But now, for some reason, Fairfax felt Sal had infringed on his territory.

''Sal was acting on my orders,'' Robert said, carefully choosing his words. ''I asked him to evaluate a man I was interested in recommending for hiring and that's what he was doing.''

''I understood from Mrs. Pierson when I took this job that I was to have full power to hire and fire.'' Fairfax spoke stiffly.

Robert tamped down his escalating annoyance. ''That doesn't mean I can't make a recommendation to you.''

''You may do that, of course.''

Something in Fairfax's manner gave Robert the feeling the man would do his damnedest to find a reason not to hire Pete if he did recommend him. Fairfax was a tin tyrant. He'd run across similar types while he was a med student and while interning—men and women jealous of their limited power. He hadn't liked any of them any better than he did Fairfax.

"I do own Pierson's Pride," Robert pointed out.

Fairfax's pale blue eyes assessed him. Had Susan told the man her son took no interest in the place? The idea that she might have riled Robert. His feelings were none of the manager's business. He didn't care for the way the man acted or the way he looked at him. Who the hell did he think he was?

Pierson's Pride belongs to me, not to Fairfax.

"Do you challenge my right to hire a vineyard worker?" Robert asked abruptly.

Fairfax's mouth tightened. "If a manager loses his authority, the job becomes impossible. I wouldn't have taken this position if I'd thought the owner would go over my head."

"You mean you'd quit if I insist rather than recommend that you hire a particular worker?"

"Exactly." Fairfax folded his arms and waited.

Robert stared at him incredulously, wondering who Fairfax thought he was bluffing. "I accept your resignation as of today," he said coldly. "Under the circumstances, I believe a month's severance pay is fair. There's no need to speak to my mother. I'll explain the situation to her."

He swung on his heel and strode to the house. Good riddance!

Susan was watering the plants in what she liked to call the reception room, off the entry. She put down the can as soon as he entered.

"I'm glad you're here," she told him. "I may have been a bit hasty last night. Laura has admitted to me that she and she alone concocted that dreadful elopement idea. Apparently Mr. Ramirez was not only not to blame but acted quite reasonably under the circumstances. Her confession gave me no choice but to reconsider my position. Perhaps I shouldn't have demanded you fire him."

Robert waved her to one of the wicker chairs and sat in the other, draping a leg over its arm. "The good news is I didn't fire Sal. I never had any intention of firing him. In fact, though he doesn't know it yet, I've decided to promote him."

She raised her eyebrows. "Promote? But isn't he already the foreman?"

"Vince Fairfax and I had a disagreement and he resigned, leaving us short a manager." He paused to let her digest that, then added, "I'm appointing Sal."

Susan drew in her breath. Her back stiffened. "A Chicano as manager of Pierson's Pride? Really, Robbie! I can't think what's gotten into you. Your father would never have dreamed of doing anything so rash."

Though he tensed inwardly, he didn't change position and he kept his voice level. "You've told me time and again I look like your side of the family. I've also heard you thank God I didn't take after my father. So why does it surprise you that I'm not behaving the way you think he might have? *I am not my father.*"

"Well, of course not, but—"

"Sal is capable, Sal knows the vineyards better than anyone else—hell, he's been running things for Fairfax right along. If I hadn't been such a blind fool I'd have made Sal manager a long time ago."

Susan leaned forward, a frown creasing her forehead, obviously girding for battle. Time to regroup.
Robert swung his leg off the chair arm, straightened and
waited for her opening salvo.

His mother opened her mouth, blinked and closed it
without saying a word. Her gaze traveled over him as if
she might be reevaluating what she saw. "What's done
is done," she said finally. Rising, she picked up the watering can and resumed tending to the plants.

*I may have won the skirmish but I've certainly been
royally dismissed,* he told himself wryly.

As he drove back to Sal's, he couldn't help wondering if he really was so very different from his father.
Hadn't they both made the mistake of getting emotion-
ally entangled with Gabaldons—his father with Estella
and he with Estella's daughter?

Was it a mistake? Robert sighed. Consumed as he was
by his need for Maya, how could he tell? All he knew was
that their affair was beyond his control. Way, way beyond. He couldn't stay away from her. His passion for
her made him understand why men would kill to be with
the woman they— He paused. Had he been about to say
loved? *Loved* was the wrong word. Wanted. The woman
they wanted.

Love was a loaded word. He didn't trust it. He knew
what he meant when he said he wanted Maya and so did
she. But love? He shook his head. Too easily said by too
many and too seldom felt. Or understood.

He preferred to say affection. Need. Liking. Those
were more explicit words. They described feelings he
understood.

After talking to Sal, Robert smiled all the way back to
the clinic, relishing his mental replay of Sal's reaction

when he heard the news—a bemused expression quickly followed by an unrestrained whoop of joy and then a rib-crushing bear hug.

I've finally done something right, Robert thought.

He decided to wait until after hours to tell Maya. Near four, because Maya was busy giving an injection to an elderly man, he asked Dolly to help a mother hold a struggling, screaming child so he could look into the boy's ears.

When he'd given the child a shot of penicillin for his inner ear infection and instructed the mother to bring him in for five more days of shots, Robert happened to notice what a tiny woman Dolly was. Not only short but with narrow shoulders and hips. Were her hips too narrow to deliver normally?

"How far along are you?" he asked her.

"Almost seven months, Doctor."

"When was your last exam?"

She thought. "I guess maybe three weeks ago."

"Did your doctor mention any problems?"

Dolly bit her lip. "She said maybe I might need a C-section 'cause I was sort of small for the baby to get through. I hope I don't."

He smiled at her. "I hope you don't, too. If you and Pete decide to stay in Thompsonville, you'd better choose a doctor in the area so you can be checked regularly."

She looked up at him shyly. "Would you be my doctor?"

He wished he could say yes. Especially since he knew she and Pete had no money. Because of that, she'd never be able to find a doctor in Thompsonville who would accept her as a patient.

"I'd like to be your doctor," he said, "but I'm an internist. I don't deliver babies. I'll be glad to see you for anything other than pregnancy but most likely you'll have to deliver at the County Hospital. Once your car is fixed you'll have no trouble getting there for appointments with one of their obstetric residents."

She tried, but failed, to mask her disappointment. "I'd like it to be you 'cause I know you're a good doctor," she said.

"Thanks for your kind words. Unfortunately, I'm no obstetrician."

Later, in the privacy of his office, he told Maya he'd made Sal the manager of Pierson's Pride.

"How wonderful!" she cried, flinging her arms around him.

He caught her to him and kissed her, deeply and thoroughly. The sweet heat of her mouth and the feel of her soft curves against him aroused him so that he forgot everything else. His hands cupped her buttocks, pressing her closer.

Not close enough. He wanted more, wanted all the wild passion he'd tasted before with her. Now. Here.

"Not here," she said breathlessly, finally breaking away.

He took a moment to return to the reality of the clinic. She was right. Not here and not now. "I'll come by after I make evening hospital rounds," he said, wishing he didn't have to part from her even for a minute.

As it turned out, they had barely an hour together at her apartment before an emergency sent him back to the hospital. An hour with Maya was never enough. Sometimes he wondered if he'd ever have enough.

The remaining weeks of August proved to be equally frustrating for Robert, with long and busy clinic days and so many after-hour emergency calls that he couldn't be with Maya even half as much as he wished.

Some things improved, though. Laura, for a welcome change, surprised everyone by behaving like a model sister and daughter during her remaining weeks at home. Still, it was a relief when his mother drove Laura up to Stanford to begin the fall quarter.

Pete, after two weeks on the job, was shaping up as careful and hardworking. He and Dolly were alone in Sal's cottage now because Sal had moved into the manager's house at Pierson's Pride. So far as Robert could tell, Sal was doing an excellent job in his new post.

Susan had no complaints; she professed to be pleased he was taking an interest in the property. He didn't disabuse her; he was enjoying the serenity at home far too much. Except for the fact he didn't have enough time alone with Maya, there was nothing to be worried or upset about. So why, Robert asked himself, did he have this sense of impending doom?

The first Sunday of September, since Pete was working, Maya picked up Dolly and drove to the local supermarket for the week's groceries. Watching Dolly descend the steps to get into the VW, Maya wondered, not for the first time, if she'd ever have a child. In a way, she envied Dolly.

Dolly and Pete hadn't agonized over whether or not to bring a child into the world; they'd just let nature take its course. As Dolly had once said, "You fall in love, you get married, then you have a baby."

It would never be that simple for her, Maya knew. Loving Robert didn't lead to marriage and she couldn't imagine ever loving another man. No marriage, no children. She admired the courage of single parents, but to her way of thinking, a child needed both a mother and a father in the home. A married mother and father.

"The baby's kicking a lot," Dolly said as she slid awkwardly into the passenger seat.

Maya put a hand to Dolly's rounded abdomen and was promptly kicked by a tiny foot. She smiled at Dolly, concealing her twinge of sadness at the very real possibility she'd never feel life growing within herself.

"I'm tired all the time lately," Dolly said, putting a hand to her back. "I guess it's a good thing I stopped working."

"In the clinic, you mean. Sal's told me how hard you've been working at cleaning and fixing up his house. He says he's never seen the place look so good."

"Sal's a good man. When he moved into the manager's house he told us we could stay in this cottage as long as we want. He won't take rent, so Pete and me, we do what we can. Pete's going to paint the kitchen next week. White, we decided. He said he never thought he'd like working in the fields but grape picking's okay and everyone's so friendly and all that he'd like to stay here. Me, I never want to go back to the city." Dolly caressed her abdomen. "I want my baby to grow up in a place like this."

"The townspeople aren't all friendly," Maya cautioned. "There's prejudice in Thompsonville."

Dolly shrugged. "No one's been mean to me."

Maya struggled to explain her point. "Usually they're not mean in the sense that they say nasty things or threaten physical harm. They just sort of look down on you or ignore you."

"It's peaceful here, anyway," Dolly said.

Maya parked in the market lot and, as they walked toward the entrance, noticed Dolly putting a hand to her back again.

"Does it hurt?" she asked.

"I guess I strained a muscle scrubbing the kitchen walls," Dolly said.

"You have to be careful not to overdo."

Dolly nodded.

After they completed their shopping and drove back to the cottage, Maya insisted on carrying in Dolly's bags of groceries. The air conditioner that cooled the kitchen and living room was on but, judging from the closed doors, none of the rest were. She'd just set the last bag on the counter by the sink when Dolly gasped.

"Oh, God, what's happening?" she cried.

Maya whirled. Blood-tinged fluid streamed down Dolly's legs, puddling on the floor. Her membranes had ruptured.

As quickly as she could, Maya helped Dolly strip off her skirt and underpants. Maya opened the first door she came to, saw a white-painted iron bedstead and led Dolly inside. She assisted her onto the bed, ordering her to lie flat.

The window air conditioner in the bedroom was not on and the room was stifling.

"My back hurts something awful." Dolly's voice was so low Maya could hardly hear her.

Aware that labor contractions were sometimes first felt as back pain, Maya laid her hand on Dolly's distended abdomen. Hard. Contracting. With an eye on her watch, she timed the contraction.

"It hurts," Dolly moaned.

The contraction lasted so long Maya knew Dolly was in active labor. She'd best call an ambulance—pronto.

As she started to turn away, she decided to check one more thing.

"Bend your knees and spread your legs apart," she ordered. When the whimpering Dolly obeyed, Maya looked to see if there was any sign of impending birth. To her horror, she saw five tiny fingers.

A malposition! In a normal delivery, the baby's head came down the birth canal first. If the buttocks or feet came first, it was still possible to deliver the child as a breech birth. But the hand meant the baby's shoulder was at the opening of the womb, making delivery impossible.

There was nothing at all Maya could do about it. Worse, she knew the baby might die before she found a way to get Dolly to a hospital. Especially since this baby was a month premature.

Don't panic, Maya admonished herself. Keep calm.

"I'll call an ambulance," she told Dolly.

She'd taken two steps when she heard the door open, then Robert's voice.

"Anyone home?"

"Robert!" she cried. "In the bedroom. Hurry!"

Moments later, Maya rushed to his car to retrieve his medical bag. She flung it onto a chest of drawers, opened the bag and pulled out a package of sterile disposable gloves. While Robert jammed them onto his hands, she found a clean sheet, placed one edge under Dolly's buttocks and spread the sheet on the bed.

Maya watched Robert take a deep breath before he reached into the birth canal with his gloved right hand. Dolly cried out.

"Take deep breaths, Dolly," he ordered.

His words made Maya realize what she should do. It was Robert's job to try to push the baby's hand back into the womb and attempt to maneuver the legs into position for a breech delivery. Her job was to help keep Dolly calm.

Holding one of Dolly's hands, she said, "Listen to me and do what I tell you. Breathe in to the count of five—one, two, three, four, five. Breathe out to the count of six." Over and over she intoned the count, fixing Dolly's attention on the breathing as best she could.

"Got it," Robert muttered after a time. "Okay, here we go."

Dolly began to grunt.

"Let her push," Robert said.

Maya lifted Dolly's hands, one at a time, to the enameled metal bars of the headboard. "Hold on to these," she said, "and push down when the doctor tells you to."

Remembering that a shoulder presentation of a baby was often the result of its mother's small pelvis, she prayed that Dolly's pelvis wasn't too narrow to allow the baby's head to pass through. If it was, the baby would die.

"Push," Robert ordered.

Sweat beaded Dolly's forehead as she obeyed; sweat ran down Robert's face as he manipulated the infant's body through the birth canal. Maya felt the heat, too, and realized the bedroom must be incubator warm. Hard on the adults but perfect for a premature baby.

"A girl. She's out!" Robert's voice rang with triumph.

He held the baby girl upside down, a gloved finger in her mouth to force out mucus. Maya saw, to her dismay, that instead of a healthy pink or red, the baby's skin had a bluish tint from lack of oxygen.

Robert laid the baby on Dolly's stomach, took the bulb syringe Maya handed him and suctioned the infant's nose and mouth.

"Get a nasal catheter from my bag," he said.

Maya found it, opened the sterile package and offered the very small catheter to him. He threaded the tube through the baby's mouth into its windpipe and used the bulb to suction out more mucus.

The tiny girl coughed—the first sound she'd made.

Robert removed the tube and tipped her upside down again. She emitted a feeble, choked wail.

Dolly, who hadn't said a word all this time, began to cry. "I thought my baby was dead," she sobbed.

By the time the afterbirth was delivered, the infant had pinked up and was crying fitfully. She was very small, a typical preemie with downy fuzz all over her and the wrinkled look of a little old lady. She couldn't be much over three pounds, Maya decided.

Robert tied the umbilical cord with sterile suture thread from his bag and cut the cord with suture scissors from the same pack. Maya wrapped the baby carefully in a clean soft towel and placed her in the crook of Dolly's arm.

The fearful wonder in Dolly's face as she gazed at her daughter brought tears to Maya's eyes.

"She may be small but she's all there," Robert assured Dolly as he stripped off his gloves. "I'll see about getting you both admitted to the hospital here in town as my patients. Since the baby's already born there shouldn't be a problem. She'll need special care for about a month, until she gains enough weight to come home. You'll need to stay in the hospital for a few days for observation because you'll run the risk of an infection."

Dolly reached her free hand toward him and he clasped it in his. "I'm going to name her Roberta," she told him. "After you."

Maya saw Robert's throat work convulsively. His voice was husky as he said, "That's the greatest honor I'll ever receive."

After the ambulance picked up mother and child, Robert told Maya he'd go home, find Pete and tell him that he was the father of a daughter. Since his clothes were blood spattered, he also needed to change. "How about lunch somewhere cool and relaxing?" he asked. "I'll stop by the hospital and then pick you up."

"At my place," she told him, remembering the groceries still in her car. "I'll clean up here and then go home." She shook her head. "I should have realized earlier that Dolly was in labor. When I saw those tiny fingers I came close to panicking, then I heard your voice and it was like the answer to a prayer. You really deserve to have that baby named after you."

"I don't mind telling you I've never been so scared in my life," he admitted. "I didn't know how the hell I was going to get the baby out alive. In my one and only month on the OB service as an intern, I never even saw a version, much less assisted with one. I'd read texts about how to perform various versions but reading about reaching inside a woman's uterus to turn a baby and actually doing it are two different things."

"She's such a tiny baby—I hope she'll be all right."

Robert grinned. "With a name like Roberta, how can she miss?"

He drove home in a euphoric mood. He'd met a challenge, he'd come through, and, because he had, a new life had been brought into the world.

He'd defied local convention by hiring Sal as Pierson's Pride's vineyard manager and it was already clear that his choice had been the right one.

And he was taking Maya to lunch. With luck they'd spend the rest of the day and the night together.

What more could a man ask?

"Somebody called," the maid told him as soon as he walked in the front door. "I left a message for you by the phone in the library."

"Thanks, Elsie," he said. "Who called?"

"Dr. Renwick, he said his name was."

Robert frowned as he walked into the library. His partner in San Francisco. What did Bill want? He'd talked to him just last Monday. Sitting at the desk, he punched in the numbers, aware that his euphoria had vanished, leaving him with the same vague sense of dread that had been plaguing him for the past several weeks.

Chapter Thirteen

Robert stood on the balcony of Bill's town house, a balcony overlooking the bay, and watched the fog gradually blot out one light after another as it drifted into San Francisco. Though he enjoyed the view and found the damp coolness of the evening refreshing after the heat of the Valley, it didn't put him in a party mood. Yet there'd been no polite way he could have turned down his partner's invitation.

"The party's to introduce Gene Fowler," Bill had said, "and to welcome *you* back, of course."

"I'm not all the way back yet," Robert had protested. In vain.

He was in San Francisco because of Bill's insistence that he drive up and meet their prospective associate, Dr. Fowler, so a decision could be made then and there. Bill was tired of carrying the workload of the practice alone and Robert didn't blame him.

So he'd come to the city, met Gene, found him personable and his credentials impressive. Just the man they needed as an associate, he assured Bill.

He should have relished a weekend free from emergency calls. Instead, he found himself restless and vaguely uneasy.

Turning away from the vista of the city, he glanced through the open sliding door at the guests, psyching himself up to go back into the room and make polite conversation. Suddenly he paused, drawing in his breath.

She drifted past the door, her dark hair floating off her bare shoulders, the straps of her red dress vivid against her creamy skin....

Her name was on his lips as he strode through the opening in the room, eager to reach her. "Maya!"

She turned her head to look at him and his heart sank. Her eyes were blue, not amber, and though she was pretty she lacked Maya's elegance of feature. Of course she couldn't be Maya—he knew Maya wasn't here.

"I'm sorry," he muttered, aware he'd inadequately concealed his disappointment. "I thought you were someone else."

"Her name's Paula Ketterman," Bill said from behind him. "Paula, this is Robert Pierson, my as-of-lately-absentee partner. You two have a lot in common—you both come from families who own vineyards."

"I rather think Dr. Pierson would prefer someone named Maya," Paula said coolly.

"Nobody here by that name," Bill said. "Anyway, after meeting you, how could he prefer someone else?"

Robert mustered up a smile for Paula. "It's a pleasure to meet you. Where are your vineyards?"

"Near Sonoma. My family owns a small winery."

"Small like in exclusive," Bill put in. "Their cellar is fantastic." He turned away to speak to another guest.

"In Thompsonville, we're mostly table grapes," Robert said, wondering why talking to this very attractive woman seemed such a chore.

"And this is picking season," Paula said. "Is that why you're an absentee doctor right now?"

"No, I pretty much leave running the vineyard to the manager."

Paula raised her eyebrows. "He must be very capable. But I can understand how your profession would keep you busy. My family is pretty much wrapped up in wine-making—both my sister and I are oenologists."

"I'm impressed."

"Don't be, I'm still learning wine-making. I'm told it takes more than a degree to become a really good oenologist, it takes a lifetime. Have you ever thought about putting in wine grapes?"

"Not seriously." He didn't choose to explain to Paula that he had never taken much of an interest in the vineyard. "If I should consider it in the future, I'll make certain to consult with you beforehand."

Out of habit, he found himself saying the right things to indicate a personal interest in her that he didn't really feel. Paula, he decided, was exactly the kind of woman his mother would choose for him—she had all the qualifications, plus the bonus of a degree in oenology.

His mother didn't understand two things. First, marriage wasn't for him, and second, when he wanted a woman, he'd do the choosing. Before he'd met Maya again, Paula might have interested him. Unfortunately, all he could see when he looked at Paula or any other woman was that none of them were Maya.

So what was he going to do about that problem when he came back to San Francisco permanently?

Maya had told herself she wouldn't sit around all weekend moping. Just because Robert had gone to the city didn't mean she had to stay home. When Sal invited her to his housewarming Saturday night, she accepted with alacrity and framed a Yaqui corn spirit print to bring along as her gift. Since he'd asked her to come early to act as his hostess, she arrived before the other guests.

Now that he'd moved into the manager's house, Sal was letting the Lueras stay in his cottage rent-free until they got on their feet financially—a wonderful break for them.

Maya had never before been inside the manager's house at Pierson's Pride. As she handed her gift to Sal, she looked around appreciatively.

"Nice going, cuz," she told him. "I can't think of anyone who deserves this more."

Sal grinned. "Never thought I'd make it here, did you?"

"Did *you?*" she countered.

"I had a hunch I might. Sooner or later Rob always comes through."

She raised an eyebrow. "Does he?"

"Yeah. Don't forget, I've known him longer than you. Takes him a while to find his bearings but he winds up heading in the right direction."

Maybe with Sal, she thought, but not with me. My way and Robert's way are as separate as north and south.

"I got a problem I need your help with, though," Sal told her. "Mrs. P. called me last night. Surprised the hell out of me."

"What's she upset about now?"

"She's not upset. What she wants is for me to organize some kind of entertainment for a fair her woman's group is putting on during the Grape Festival."

The Thompsonville Grape Festival was always the third weekend in September. Maya couldn't remember a time when there hadn't been a festival to celebrate the harvesting of grapes.

There was always a parade with bands, floats and an evening barbecue in the town park. All the merchants donated raffle prizes and the kids usually ran races and played games.

"Why is Mrs. Pierson having this fair?" she asked.

"She said her group's trying to raise money for La Raza Clínica."

Maya stared at him, not believing her ears. "For *what?*"

"You heard me. So she'd like some old-time Chicano entertainment as part of the fair."

"Is that what she told you?"

"You know better. She said she wanted 'the culture of my people represented.' I sure as hell couldn't refuse, so now what?"

"You're asking me to help?"

"Who else?"

"Mrs. Pierson wouldn't want me associated with her fair in any way, shape or form."

"If you don't tell her and I don't tell her, how's she to know?"

Maya sighed. "Okay, but I have a feeling I'll regret this."

Sal grinned and hugged her. "We'll start planning tomorrow—tonight's for fun. Come on, I'll give you a tour of *mi casa* before the others show."

The three-bedroom house, adobe with a Spanish tile roof, was built like an old-fashioned Californio hacienda with the living quarters around a courtyard full of flowering shrubs and fruit trees.

"Sal, it's charming," she said enthusiastically. "I'd like to live here myself."

"Is that a proposal?" Sal asked, smiling. "If it is, this'll be my second this summer."

"You shouldn't make fun of poor Laura."

"If I don't joke about it, I might get to believing she meant what she said." His tone switched from teasing to somber. "And where does that leave me?" Sadness darkened his eyes. "You know, I miss her."

Maya looked at him in dismay. Had she been wrong in believing Sal's fondness for Laura was that of a brother or a father? Did he feel something different? Had rejecting Laura hurt him as much as it had her?

"It's hell to get mixed up with Piersons," she said.

Sal half smiled. "At least Rob's no kid. Laura—" He shook his head. "*Basta*. Enough. I think I heard a car— Maybe it's our mystery guest. Let's go see."

For a moment Maya didn't recognize the slim, medium-tall man walking up the stone path toward the house. Then she realized she knew him but that he'd changed.

"Dr. Halago!" she exclaimed as he entered the house. "I had no idea you were in town. Or that you'd grown a beard!"

"Just Joe, please," he said, taking her hand. "I've been hearing what a good choice I made when I hired you, Maya. Too bad I was laid low before we had a chance to work together. That's a pleasure I'm looking forward to."

The glint in his eye had nothing to do with hearing she was a good nurse, Maya thought as she smiled at him. She enjoyed being admired by an attractive man—what woman didn't?—but what could come of it? True, Joe Halago, even with his post-op pallor, was handsome. She liked him as a person and admired him for his dedication to helping their people. He was really everything she could want in a man—but he had one flaw she couldn't overlook.

He wasn't Robert.

"When are you coming back to the clinic?" she asked, withdrawing her hand.

"On Monday, for half a day. I feel good enough to work full-time but my surgeon gives the orders and, after two times on the OR table, I listen. He says half a day every other day for a week, then half-time for at least another week. We'll see. I know Rob must be chomping at the bit to return to his own practice."

"Dr. Pierson's in San Francisco this weekend," Maya said. "Does he know you're back in Thompsonville?"

Joe shook his head. "I doubt it. Didn't know for sure until Friday that my doctor was going to let me start working even half days. I thought I'd surprise everyone by just showing up on Monday, but then I met Sal at the post office and got invited to this housewarming." He smiled, his teeth white against his dark beard and mustache. "And here *you* are, even prettier than I remembered."

Sal, who'd been greeting three men carrying musical instruments, turned to Maya and Joe. "Did you bring your guitar, Doc?" he asked.

"It's in the car," Joe said.

"If you want to sit in with the guys—" Sal gestured to the three musicians "—feel free."

The trio nodded as one man. "Me, I hear you play last year, Doc," the accordionist said. "I say then you pluck those strings better than my brother here." He clapped the guitarist on the shoulder.

"We missed you, Doc," the guitarist said. "That new guy, he doctors pretty good but he don't play guitar and he don't sing."

Other arrivals, hearing him, added their own comments. In no time she and Joe were surrounded by people insisting that Doc play and sing for them.

Finally persuaded, Joe brought in his instrument, tuned it up and struck a few chords. Maya recognized an old Mexican love song about a deserted lover with a broken heart.

In a pleasing baritone, Joe sang the words as though he meant each and every one, his audience, with his encouragement, joining in on the chorus.

"Su corazón es mi corazón	Your heart is my heart
Una vez, nada má	One time, one more.
Mi corazón es su corazón	My heart is your heart
Por siempre jamás...."	Forever and more....

When he finished they called for more but he shook his head, smiling. "I came to this party to dance with pretty women. How can I dance and play at the same time?"

Maya danced with Joe more than once. She found him fun, appreciated his musical talent and enjoyed the dancing, but she wasn't able to really abandon herself to the music and the laughter.

He apparently sensed this because near midnight he drew her into a secluded corner of the courtyard. "I don't like to trespass so I have to ask. I get the feeling you're involved with someone else. Rob?"

She knew one or more of the guests must have warned him. Unable to find the right words, she merely nodded.

Joe shrugged. "Bad timing on my part, good timing on his. I hope things work out for you, I really do. But if not . . ." He didn't finish in words. Instead he kissed her lightly and quickly, his beard brushing softly across her face.

She understood what he meant—that he'd be around after Robert left—but all the kiss did was remind her of how different she felt when Robert kissed her and how much she missed him.

Later, Maya took care to leave the party unobtrusively. She'd come alone and, though she thought Joe understood her feelings, she didn't want to take the chance he might offer to see her home.

On Sunday Sal rang her doorbell at noon. She handed him a can from the six-pack of cold beer she kept in her refrigerator for his visits and sat opposite him at the kitchen table with a glass of orange juice.

"Got any cultural thoughts?" he asked after taking a long draft of beer.

"For one, why not ask Joe Halago to play? He's really good."

"He was kind of taken with you, cuz, *no es verdad?*"

She wouldn't lie to Sal but she didn't mean to tell him what had gone on between her and Joe, either. "I thought you came to discuss culture."

"Yeah, that, too. What about an artist? I mean some guy who'd paint pictures during the fair—bullfights, dancers with castanets, like that. I know a guy who's not too bad. He could sell some of his work besides raffling off a couple for the clinic.''

''Sounds great.''

They discussed the pros and cons of combos, strolling guitarists and dancers until finally Maya had what she thought of as a brilliant idea.

''Why don't you dress up in your Californio don outfit and do something dramatic on horseback?'' she asked Sal. ''What did the *vaqueros* do for fun in those days?''

''You mean besides setting up bull-and-bear fights to the death and galloping past chickens buried in the dirt up to their necks, leaning sideways in the saddle and snatching the chicken with one hand?''

''Ugh. I take it no animal survived any of those dangerous encounters. Let's forego the real for something fake, something showy but not fatal to man or beast.''

''On horseback?''

She nodded.

''I'll think about it,'' he said. ''Maybe I can come up with what we need. When Laura was a kid, we used to play a kind of game where I'd be on horseback and she'd stand by the road and wait for me to ride by, scoop her up and sit her in front of me on the saddle. I was careful not to ride too fast so it wasn't really dangerous.'' He shook his head, smiling to himself. ''God, how she loved that game. Used to drive me crazy with wanting to play it.''

''You're thinking of trying that trick with some other child?''

''I don't know.'' Sal spoke as though his mind were a thousand miles away. Or perhaps years away, in the past.

After long moments he shifted his shoulders and glanced at her. "Heard from Rob?" he asked.

She shook her head. "He said when he left he'd call me when he got back. That'll probably be sometime this evening."

Sal nodded. They discussed possibilities for the fair for another hour before he left. Maya did her best to find chores to occupy her time, hating to think she was putting herself on hold until Robert's call. The hours dragged by, afternoon slipped into evening and evening darkened into night. Was he home yet? Had he forgotten to call?

She decided she'd wait until eleven and then go to bed. At ten-thirty the doorbell rang. Her heart leaped.

"Robert?" she called through the door as she reached for the chain.

Silence. Maya froze. Who was it?

"You don't know me," a woman's voice said. "I'm looking for *La Curandera.*"

Maya opened the door and saw a dark-haired woman in her forties. "Come in," she said.

The woman shook her head. "I'm Rita, Mrs. Guerrera's daughter-in-law. She's real bad but she won't go to the hospital. She wants you. She says you can cure her. So I come to get you."

Maya remembered Mrs. Guerrera. A woman in her eighties with a diagnosis of congestive heart failure, a condition that was being treated by medication and observed by follow-up clinic visits every two weeks. It occurred to her that she hadn't seen Mrs. Guerrera in the clinic for more than a month.

"Has your mother-in-law been taking her medicine?" Maya asked.

Rita shrugged. "Who can tell? She won't let Pepe or me give her the pills. She says she takes them but who knows? Don't eat no salty stuff, the doctor tells her, but if we don't watch her real close, she sneaks it."

"I'll come with you and take a look at her," Maya said. "But if she's as bad as it sounds, she'll have to go to the hospital."

Rita rolled her eyes. "She's stubborn, that one. Won't listen to a word I say and not too much of what Pepe tells her."

When Maya reached her VW, she saw with dismay that the right front tire was all but flat.

"You ride in my car," Rita offered. "Me, I don't mind bringing you home—you're doing us a big favor by coming. My mother-in-law don't trust no one but *La Curandera.*"

Maya found Mrs. Guerrera propped up against pillows on a couch in the living room of her small house.

"She stays out here 'cause we don't have no air conditioners in the bedrooms," her son Pepe said. "Mama can't breathe so good."

Maya knelt beside the couch and took Mrs. Guerrera's hand in hers, finding a rapid, thready pulse. The old woman's skin was bluish and she grunted with each breath—alarming signs that showed her lungs were rapidly filling with fluid.

"Mrs. Guerrera," she said. "You're very sick. I can't cure you. You need help fast. Help only a doctor in a hospital can give you."

Mrs. Guerrera clutched at Maya's hand and stared at her.

"You must go to a hospital," Maya said firmly.

"If you take me," the old woman gasped, "I go. No ambulance."

Maya nodded and hurried to the phone. She called the Pierson house and was coolly informed by Susan that Dr. Pierson was not in town. Afraid no local doctor would see a clinic patient, Maya decided she had no choice but to find Joe Halago. Luckily, Sal had his number. Joe agreed to meet her at the local ER.

She sat in the back seat, propping up Mrs. Guerrera while Pepe drove to the I. R. Thompson emergency room.

Joe immediately gave Mrs. Guerrera an injection of morphine and started oxygen per mask. But when he tried to have her admitted to ICU, he was told the hospital's small intensive care unit was full.

By the time Mrs. Guerrera was admitted to the County Hospital ICU in Bakersfield and Maya and Joe returned to Thompsonville, it was well past midnight.

As Joe's car turned in Maya's drive, she started to say she'd see him later in the day at the clinic but stopped before the first word left her lips, staring at the blue sports car parked behind her VW. In the illumination of Joe's headlights, she watched Robert slide from the car to stand facing them, scowling.

Joe stopped. "Looks like old Rob's waiting up for us," he told Maya.

He turned off the motor and they both got out. Joe strode toward Robert, his hand extended. Considering Robert's glare, Maya wondered if he'd shake Joe's hand.

What on earth was wrong with him?

Joe sure as hell hadn't wasted any time, Robert thought as he reached a reluctant hand to meet Joe's.

"I guess I'm not going to get to surprise anyone," Joe said, sounding impossibly cheerful.

"You surprised me." Robert couldn't help the curl of anger in his voice.

Joe blinked, then glanced sideways at Maya, who stood apart from the two of them. Bringing his gaze back to Robert, he said, "Cool down, *amigo,* or you'll get ulcers, like I did." He smiled at them both. "See you tomorrow. Good night, Maya. Thanks for the help."

Walking quickly to his car, he got in and drove away.

"You weren't particularly welcoming to your friend," Maya said. "At least I thought he was your friend."

"I've been here since eleven," Robert said. "I've had time to change your flat tire and listen to fifty tapes. As well as have a few second thoughts. About friends."

She folded her arms across her chest. "What *is* the matter with you?"

He knew he was overreacting and tried to take Joe's advice. The trouble was his anger had percolated too long for him to cool off easily. First he'd merely been impatient when he called Maya at eleven and nobody answered the phone. He'd tried to reach Sal to ask if he knew where Maya was, but there was no answer at Sal's, either.

Impatience escalated into annoyance when he drove here and found her car but not her. Where was she? Why wasn't she in her apartment? Hadn't he told her he'd be home Sunday night? Hadn't he said he'd call her when he got in?

After all, he'd turned down a chance to get better acquainted with an interesting woman in San Francisco. The least Maya could do was be where he expected her to be when he returned.

As the minutes passed and she didn't come home, he got angry. It was late—where was she? What could she be doing? But, upset though he was, he hadn't in his heart of hearts believed she could possibly be with another man.

Not until Joe Halago stepped from his car.

"I didn't realize you and Joe were so well acquainted," he said, trying to speak calmly. And failing.

Maya raised her chin. "There are undoubtedly a lot of things you don't know."

Two steps brought him close enough to grip her shoulders. Taking a deep breath, he restrained an impulse to shake her. He was an adult, not an impulsive teenager unable to control himself.

"Why?" he asked.

"Why what?" Her tone challenged him.

"Why weren't you home?"

She jerked free. "If you'd behaved like a normal human being instead of like some avenging angel, we would have told you."

We. The two of them. His heart suddenly felt as heavy as lead. Told him what? He wasn't sure he wanted to know.

"After all," she added, "Mrs. Guerrera *is* your patient."

Robert stared at her. Mrs. Guerrera? What was Maya talking about?

"She filled up with fluid," Maya said. "Acute pulmonary edema. Her relatives came for me when she refused to go to the hospital."

As Robert listened to Maya's account of what had happened, a mixture of relief and shame replaced his anger. In his jealousy, it hadn't occurred to him that someone might have asked for *La Curandera*'s help.

"You really glowered at poor Joe," Maya finished. "If looks could kill, he'd be lying stone-cold dead in my driveway."

"I didn't know he was back," Robert muttered. "I didn't expect to see him." He left "with you" unsaid.

"Some greeting you gave him."

Robert couldn't blame her for being upset with him. "I guess I was a bit hasty but, damn it, Maya, when I saw you with another man—" He broke off, shaking his head. "I meant tonight to be different than it's turned out to be."

"Through no fault of mine." Her tone was still huffy.

He smiled wryly. "I suppose you're convinced I haven't changed at all in eleven years."

"Have you?" she asked.

He held his hands toward her, palms upward. "Considering how evil my thoughts were tonight, I behaved quite well. Positively restrained, don't you think?"

The corners of her mouth twitched as though she were suppressing a smile and he took heart. "*Restrained* wouldn't be my choice of word. Were your thoughts really evil?"

"I'm afraid so. There never was and never will be a woman who makes me as crazy as you do, Maya." He touched her cheek in a tentative caress, then ran his thumb along her lips. "Still mad at me?"

"I ought to be."

"But you're not." He couldn't recall ever wanting to kiss her as badly as he did right now.

She nipped his thumb. "If I'm not, we're both crazy."

He needed no more encouragement. Wrapping his arms around her, he held her close. "Takes one to know one," he murmured.

Chapter Fourteen

Maya strolled along the grassy verge of Tule Creek where eucalyptus, willow and ash trees hugged both sides of the stream that ran through Veteran's Park. Strung between tree branches were white banners with deep purple lettering that proclaimed Thompsonville Grape Festival.

Picnicking family groups gathered at the tables and benches set up under the trees. Later comers made do with folding chairs brought from home and blankets spread on the grass wherever trees offered shade. Even in September, the noon Valley sun shone hot and strong.

Maya paused to gaze at a smaller banner hanging from the slanted roof of the park's large lean-to shelter. It read Benefit Fair for La Raza Clínica.

Inside the shelter, people crowded around booths that sold a variety of articles—crafts, food and drink, books, plants, T-shirts with the Grape Festival logo and various other collectibles. To either side of the shelter, others patronized large umbrella-shaded tables piled with flea market bric-a-brac.

She was here to enjoy herself. She refused to allow a single negative thought inside her head. Today was for fun and she wouldn't let herself remember that, now that Joe was back and working, Robert was due to leave at the end of the month. If she permitted herself to brood over that, how could she enjoy anything?

The smell of spicy food from the shelter reminded her she was hungry so she started for the booths. A woman's voice called her name.

"Maya!"

She turned to see a group of teenagers sprawled in the shade under a tree and Laura, on her feet, running toward her. Laura threw her arms around Maya, hugging her.

"It's so great to see you again," she said. "I never got to really say goodbye."

Maya hugged her in return. "You're home for the festival, I guess."

"I wouldn't miss the grape festival for anything."

"You look marvelous. College must agree with you."

Laura smiled and smoothed her white sundress. "Like, it's okay."

"I was thinking of getting something to eat. Want to join me?"

"Sure." As they walked toward the booths, Laura said, "The show this evening sounds like fun."

About to tell her how hard Sal had been working to make it come off, Maya decided not to mention his name.

"The combo's good," she said instead. "And some of the dancers are remarkable."

Sal had crossed cultures to set up a program of ethnic dances, drawing on the people who used the clinic, and the last she'd heard he'd found groups to perform Mexican, Ecuadorean, African and Vietnamese dances.

They bought tacos at one of the booths, authentic tasting, though the pretty blond woman who sold them was certainly not Chicana. She looked familiar but Maya couldn't place her until Laura introduced them.

"Julie, Maya Najero. Maya, Julie Symond."

"Oh, yes," Julie said before Maya could speak. "Weren't you at Susan's party?"

Maya nodded. She knew now where she'd seen Julie before. Rushing up to Robert at that party. Kissing him. She'd never told him how jealous she'd been.

"Maya works with my brother at La Raza Clínica," Laura said.

"How nice." Julie's bored tone made it clear she didn't think Maya worth bothering about. "See you later, Laura," she said as she turned away to help another customer.

They strolled away from the booth. "I gather Julie's an old friend of your brother's," Maya said between bites of her taco.

"A couple of years ago he took her out a lot but then he sort of lost interest. Rob's like that." She shot Maya a sideways glance. "Or he used to be, anyway."

Maya managed what she hoped was a believable smile. "He's certainly made it clear he's not the marrying kind."

"Like Sal."

Maya had been wondering if and when Sal's name would come up. She eyed Laura warily.

Laura laughed. "Don't worry. Like, I'm over all that kid stuff."

She sounded as though she meant it. "Let's get a soda," Maya said, changing the subject.

As they stood under a nearby tree, sipping from straws, Laura identified the women at the booths. Maya was surprised to find so many doctors' wives among them. She said so.

"Yeah, they're in my mom's garden club. Mom said this fair was the camel's nose under the tent—whatever she meant by that." Laura shrugged. "Mom's a world-class persuader. She talks people into things and then makes them feel like it's their idea. You know? She's done it to Rob and me all our lives. Only I caught on sooner than he did. He may be a doctor but in some ways Rob can be kind of, you know, dumb."

"It was good of your mother to arrange the benefit," Maya said.

Laura glanced at her. "You don't really think Mom did this for the clinic, do you? She doesn't care about the clinic at all. Like, she's doing it for Rob 'cause she figures maybe he'll stay home longer if the town starts to support La Raza Clínica. She knows he's upset about the local docs refusing to help and this is her way to sort of gently force them to reconsider by getting their wives involved. Mom would do anything to keep Rob at Pierson's Pride—she's always felt he belongs there."

Maya remained silent, wondering if selfishness was all that had prompted Susan. But, since the clinic would benefit, did it really matter?

Guitar music drifted closer. Laura turned as the strolling player approached, wearing a white ruffled shirt, black pants and a bright red cummerbund. "Hey, that's Dr. Halago! I didn't know he played guitar."

"He's very good," Maya said. "Would you believe he sings, too?"

"He looks really cute with a beard."

Cute wasn't the word she'd choose but Maya nodded.

Joe saw her, smiled and, still strumming, walked toward them. When he reached their patch of shade he paused, segued into a slower tune and began to sing.

"Yo te quiero mucho..."

"He's looking right at you," Laura whispered. "He's like, singing about how much he loves you."

Maya shook her head. "It's just a song," she said in a low tone.

Maya was grateful when people began to gather around Joe, cutting him off from her and Laura. "I could use some ice cream," she said, drifting toward the booths again.

Laura followed her. "He *was* singing to you," she insisted. "I could tell."

"Who was singing to whom?" Robert's voice came from behind her, startling Maya.

"Oh, hi, Rob," Laura said. "Dr. Halago's being a strolling guitar player." She gestured toward the tree. "And he was singing a love song to Maya, only she doesn't believe me."

"I don't doubt he was. My old *amigo*'s no fool." Though Robert's words were said lightly, a dark undercurrent flowed beneath them.

Maya shifted her shoulders uneasily. Robert and Joe seemed to be good friends, but since Joe had come back part-time at the clinic, it wasn't the same for her. She worked well enough with him but his presence made a difference in the way she and Robert interacted, even on the days Joe didn't come in. Tension had replaced their easy camaraderie.

Laura's eyes darted from Robert to her and back. "Could be you've got a rival, big brother," she said, grinning.

"Could be you should get lost," Robert told her, his tone only half-kidding.

Laura pretended to cringe away. "I'm outta here!"

"It looks like your mother has a good thing going with this fair," Maya said after Laura wandered off.

He nodded. "The clinic will prosper."

"Have you noticed how many of the local doctors' wives are manning the booths?"

Robert glanced toward the shelter. "Mother has a way about her, that's for sure. But I don't see any of the doctors—and I don't expect to see them here any more than I expect them to suddenly start accepting clinic patients."

Maya was surprised at his pessimism. "Not yet, maybe, but don't underestimate the power of wives," she said.

He raised his eyebrows.

"Just wait," she told him. "Your mother's no fool."

To find herself not only admiring Susan Pierson but actually praising her disconcerted Maya. Not that she thought Susan was doing this because she believed in the clinic— No, Laura was most likely right about Susan's selfish motives. But, in arranging the benefit, Susan had tapped into the unselfishness of others to the ultimate good of the community.

How ironic, Maya thought. Our reasons may be different, but for once Susan and I have the same goals— the improvement of community relations. And, admit it, we both want Robert to stay in Thompsonville.

"I don't want to wait—I'd rather spend the afternoon alone with you," Robert said. "Preferably in some cool, secluded spot. Unfortunately, Sal roped me—and I mean that literally—into a lariat contest later so I need to practice. Care to come and watch?"

Maya smiled. "I didn't know you were that good with a rope."

"I was pretty fair once but there's not a hell of a lot of demand for a lassooing doctor."

"I'll watch as long as I'm not expected to applaud."

"No applause necessary. I'll be happy if you manage to control your laughter."

They were on their way to Robert's car when his mother stopped them.

"There you are, my dear," she said, her gaze on Maya.

My dear? Was being patronized any better than being ignored? Or falsely accused?

"I hope you have a few minutes to spare," Susan went on, "because I'd like to introduce you to the women who are helping make this little fair a success."

Maya nodded politely, keeping her resentment hidden. What did putting up with a few minutes of condescending smiles mean if it benefited the clinic?

The women didn't actually look alike, Maya knew that, but after the first few handshakes, their faces blurred one into the other. They all seemed to be light-haired—blond or gray—and dressed in subdued colors.

When she'd finished the introductions, Susan put her arm lightly around Maya's shoulders, startling her momentarily.

"We've decided to set up a women's auxiliary for the clinic," Susan told her. "You've met the nucleus of the group and I hope you'll want to help us plan how we best can be of assistance. Alicia here has offered to start a volunteer committee since she understands the clinic is chronically short of help.''

Maya looked at the blond woman Susan indicated and desperately tried to recall Alicia's last name.

"Alicia," Susan went on, "is a trained pediatric nurse who already volunteers in the I. R. Thompson newborn nursery.''

Townsend, Maya thought triumphantly, having gotten the clue she needed. Dolly had told her about Alicia Townsend.

"Thank you, Mrs. Townsend," Maya said. "I know you've been of great help to one of the clinic patients already—a preemie in the hospital nursery.''

Alicia's smile was warm and genuine. "Little Bobbie May Luera, you mean. She's a sweetheart. I'll miss her when she goes home. Do you mind if I call you and talk over a volunteer program?''

"I'd be happy to help in any way I can," Maya said, moved by Alicia's obvious sincerity. "The money all of you are raising today is greatly appreciated but we really do need volunteers, too.''

Susan Pierson gave Maya's shoulders a little squeeze before releasing her. "I'm sure we'll get along together very well," she said.

As Maya walked away to rejoin Robert, she pondered Susan's last remark. Susan must have been speaking of the newly formed auxiliary when she said "we," because certainly she and Maya would have no other reason to come in contact with each other.

Alicia's friendliness and the apparent eagerness of the other women to volunteer to help at the clinic not only had surprised Maya but had shaken her to her roots.

Donating money or raising it for charity was one thing, but these women were offering themselves—

women she'd believed had prejudice so bred into their bones that nothing could change them.

It unsettled her to find she'd been wrong. That, actually, she'd been more prejudiced against them than they were against her people. Why, she hadn't even bothered to try to tell them apart!

Her grandfather would be ashamed of her. After his many reminders that all people were one with the earth and with each other, why was that lesson so hard to keep in mind.

When she told Robert why his mother had asked her to meet the women, he shook his head. "It won't work. They'll show up once or twice and then defect."

Maya didn't agree. For some reason she had faith in these women Susan had recruited. "Your mother's got a keen eye for quality," she said.

He glanced at her, obviously astonished. "I thought you didn't like her."

"I'm not so sure that I do. But I respect her."

They drove to Pierson's Pride in Robert's sports car and parked near the barn.

Robert's efforts with a rope soon attracted two of the workers. At first they watched in silence but, after a particularly skillful twist, both shouted *"Bravo!"* Having approved, they then felt free to offer criticism—some of it helpful. It was obvious to Maya that the workers didn't stand in awe of Robert. More, that they liked him.

When he finished practicing, the two men, Luis and Curilo, walked with them to the car, giving last minute tips about how loose the knot should be and how relaxed the rope-wielder.

"I guess I won't make a total fool of myself," he told her as they drove away.

"I can't imagine you ever doing that."

"Not even when you've seen me do it?"

She grinned. "Only in front of me—not a crowd."

By the time they returned to the park, a track had been roped off for the horsemanship show. Robert joined three others, all with ropes coiled over a shoulder, near a ring marked *Por las Reatas*. For the lariats.

Rather than stand and wait for the contest to begin, Maya looked for Sal. She found him saddling Padrino near the creek.

"Good thing I waited to put on this don costume," he told her. "It's hot as hell."

Sal had decided that using a real child was too dangerous so a vineyard worker's mother had made a doll for him. He had it propped against a tree. Black yarn hair, black button eyes and a wide red smile peeked out from under a child-size sombrero. The doll was dressed much like Joe was—white ruffled shirt, black pants, red sash at the waist. Maya admired the detail the woman had put into making it.

"Want me to carry Don Quixote for you?" she asked.

"Why do women always name everything?" he asked in return.

"That's obvious. So we know what to call it."

He shook his head. "You can carry him if you want. His size makes him awkward but he's not heavy."

"Are you as nervous as Robert?" she asked.

"More. I hope to hell I don't fall flat on my face."

"And here I thought all dons were macho types."

He snorted and turned back to Padrino.

As Maya carried the doll toward the track, she encountered stares and questions. Laura appeared and fell into step beside her.

"What's that supposed to be?" Laura asked.

"Don't you recognize Don Quixote?"

"Not out of his working armor. These must be his dress clothes."

"Don Quixote belongs to Sal," Maya said. "He's going to ride past, grab the doll off the ground and set it on the saddle in front of him."

"When I was a kid he used to do that with me!" Laura cried.

"Making you both more *loco* than I thought. Anyway, he came to his senses and realized that risking a child's welfare for the sake of a trick was out of the question."

"Sal never dropped *me*."

Maya rolled her eyes. "Chances are he won't drop Don Quixote, either, but if he does, no harm's done."

At the track one of Sal's helpers took the doll from Maya and propped it carefully against two stakes, then he and a companion patrolled the narrow track to make sure spectators were behind the ropes.

In the lariat ring to the left of the track, a dark-haired man twirled his *reata*. Seeing that Robert's turn hadn't come yet, Maya returned her attention to the track. Laura, she noticed, now stood opposite her, behind the ropes on the right-hand side of the track, talking to friends. Because the doll was on that side, Laura had the best view, but Maya didn't want to miss seeing Robert's rope tricks so she stayed where she was.

Catching Robert's eye, she waved and he pushed through the crowd to join her, carrying his rope. "Still another guy before me," he said. "Might as well watch Sal."

As they waited, Robert fiddled with his rope, checking and rechecking the knot. Men, like boys, always seemed to be setting up some feat or other to measure themselves against. Far fewer women were guilty of this. A gender difference? Maya wondered.

The thud of hooves alerted her and she craned her neck to look down the track. The Californio don costume, like a tuxedo in modern-day wear, changed Sal's appearance from casual to formal, giving him a regal look as he trotted toward them on Padrino.

A gasp from the woman next to her pulled Maya's attention from Sal.

"Oh my God, he'll be killed!" the woman cried, pointing.

A toddler on Maya's side had ducked under the ropes and was in the middle of the track, intent on grabbing the doll. Horse and rider were almost upon him. Before Maya could move, Laura squirmed through the ropes on the opposite side and flung herself toward the little boy. At the same time, Robert swung his lariat. The loop settled over the child. Robert drew it taut about the boy's waist and hauled him to safety.

Seeing this, Laura tried to scramble back to the ropes but her ankle twisted and she stumbled onto her knees. The crowd drew in its breath as the horse loomed over her. There wasn't room for Sal to swerve enough to miss her.

Sal, already leaning from the saddle, swerved Padrino as much as he could, reached out and grabbed Laura around the waist, lifted her and swung himself and Laura upright into the saddle, settling her in front of him.

The crowd went wild. Sal slowed Padrino, turned him and trotted back, bending to scoop up the doll as he passed. He rode down the track toward the creek with a smiling Laura in front of him, holding the doll as she waved to the cheering crowd.

Robert grasped Maya's arm and ran interference as they pushed through the crowd. They reached the creek ahead of most of the others, in time to see Sal reach up to lift Laura off Padrino. Maya ran toward them. By the time she got there, Sal had set Laura on her feet and released her but he was still staring into her eyes as though mesmerized.

"How much older do I have to get?" Laura asked him in a whisper so faint that Maya wasn't entirely certain she heard right.

If Sal answered, Maya didn't hear. She threw her arms around Sal and hugged him before hugging Laura. Then Robert, his arm around his sister, clapped Sal on the shoulder.

"Un caballero magnífico," he said.

"Is the kid okay?" Sal asked him.

"Maybe a few bruises but he's fine," Robert said. "When I handed him to his mother he was crying because he didn't get the doll."

Laura, doll clutched to her, said, "Don Quixote's *mine.*"

Sal smiled. "No argument. You earned him."

And then excited and admiring people closed in around them. Laura was swept off by her friends and Sal surrounded by his.

Once Maya and Robert fought their way free, he said, "After that exhibition, anything the fair could offer would be an anticlimax. Let's go somewhere cool—like my house—and relax."

Maya wondered if he realized this was the first time, not counting the party, that he'd invited her home. "Sounds good to me—but let's drive separately so I don't have to leave my car parked here."

When she pulled behind his car in the driveway at Pierson's Pride, Robert was talking to Luis, one of the workers she'd met earlier.

"I didn't stay for the lariat contest," he said.

"Maybe not," she put in, coming up to them, "but in my opinion you won, hands down." She went on to tell Luis how Robert had saved the child.

"Sal was the real hero," Robert said, and told that story.

Luis grinned. "It's good to work for brave men."

After Maya and Robert left him, they walked hand in hand to the side porch. Robert pushed open the door and they entered. He paused before reaching the closed door to the house.

"Do you mind sitting out here? It's one of my favorite places."

Maya looked around at the chintz-covered chairs and couch. The screened porch, shaded by an enormous valley oak, seemed pleasantly cool after the heat of the sun. "It certainly looks comfortable."

"Good. Sit down and I'll find us something to drink. Don't expect orange juice."

She sank into one of the chairs, relaxing, letting the tension induced by the near accident at the fair ebb away. A warm breeze drifted through the screens, carrying the faintly sweet scent of grapes drying in the sun as they shriveled into raisins.

She knew that all but a few of the table grapes had been harvested. The rest went to the winery or became raisins. Soon the long hot days would end, bringing the welcome cool of autumn. The grape leaves would yellow and fall, baring the vines for the pruners' shearing.

And then the cold tule fogs would settle in, blanketing the Valley in gray winter. And she would be alone.

"Is lemonade all right?" Robert's voice startled her from her unhappy musing.

"Fine." She started to reach for one of the glasses but he set them both on the marble-topped table in front of the couch.

"That chair you're in isn't big enough for two," he pointed out.

She smiled and moved to the couch. He sat next to her and draped an arm over her shoulders, pulling her close to his side. She leaned her head against him and sighed with pleasure.

"I want you to come to San Francisco with me," he said.

Maya sat up, easing away to face him, her heart pounding. "For a visit, you mean?"

"No. I don't want you in Thompsonville and me in the city. I want you there, living with me."

He was asking her to live with him. God knows she was tempted. But how could she? Taking a deep breath, she said, "I have an obligation to the clinic. I can't desert them."

"That's no problem. Give them notice, stay on until they find a replacement and then join me."

Maya bit her lip. How could she make him understand? "My obligation is not just to the clinic but to my people. They need me here."

He set his jaw. "In other words, the clinic's more important to you than I am."

"No! That just isn't true."

"Then come with me."

"I can't."

He gripped her shoulders. "There must be clinics and hospitals in the city that need you as badly as La Raza Clínica. What's wrong with working at one of them?"

"I grew up with the people here." Tears misted her eyes. "They're a part of me. I became a nurse so I could come back and help them. Your father understood. Why can't you?"

He thrust her away from him. "My father! What's he got to do with you and me?"

She rose from the couch and crossed her arms over her breasts. "He was your father and my friend. He helped me and now it's my turn to help my people." Staring at the implacable sheen of his brown eyes, she knew she was wasting her time trying to explain how she felt. Anger roughened her voice. "It's easy enough for you to turn your back on Joe and the clinic—they mean nothing to you. For me, it's different."

"Joe." He leaped to his feet and stood facing her, fists clenched. "He's the real reason you want to stay here, isn't he? Why not admit the truth?"

She stared at him in disbelief. "You're impossible!"

Turning toward the door, she took no more than two steps before he grasped her arm and whirled her around. "Are you in love with him?" he demanded.

Angry and upset as she was, she almost laughed. How could he fail to know by now that Robert Pierson was the only man she could ever love?

"No matter what I say you won't believe me," she said hotly. "What's the use of trying to convince you of anything?"

"There's only one way to convince *you*," he said, and yanked her into his arms.

His kiss devoured her, leaving her drained and weak-kneed. With all her heart she wanted to stay in his arms but the triumphant glint in his eyes stiffened her wobbly will. She forced herself to pull free.

"It's time I left." Skirting past him, she stalked through the door.

All the way to her VW, she thought he'd follow. He did not. She started the car, circled and pulled away without any sign of Robert. He was letting her go.

Swallowing did nothing to relieve the lump in her throat as she eased her car from the driveway onto the main road. On the drive home she kept blinking back tears but by the time she reached her apartment she was crying so hard the world was blurred.

She stumbled up the steps, managed to unlock the door after three tries, curled onto the couch and sobbed until no tears were left. As she mopped her wet face, she felt the cool touch of her silver bracelet against her heated cheeks. A sudden vision of the silver dream fence that had barred her from Robert flashed into her mind.

This time she'd shut herself away from him forever.

Chapter Fifteen

On Sunday morning the phone woke Maya. Groggy with sleep, she stumbled from the bedroom to answer it, hoping despite herself that it was Robert.

"This is Beatrice Reinholt," a woman's voice informed her.

Maya blinked, desperately trying to place the name. Her landlady!

"I'll be back next week as planned," Mrs. Reinholt went on, "but I wanted to alert you that I'm having some boxes sent on ahead. Would you be a dear and store them in your apartment for me?"

Maya agreed and hung up. She looked at the clock and was amazed to see it was almost noon. No wonder, since she hadn't fallen asleep until dawn. She took a deep breath, stretching, trying to erase the fuzziness from her mind and at the same time trying to prevent sadness from creeping in. She mustn't allow her obsession with Robert to affect every facet of her life.

This morning Bobbie May was coming home from the hospital and she'd promised Dolly she'd be over to help get the baby settled in.

Though she'd never felt less like visiting anyone, Maya showered and dressed. She forced herself to swallow a few gulps of orange juice but couldn't eat anything. At the moment she couldn't imagine ever being hungry again.

When she arrived at the Lueras', Pete let her in and followed her into the baby's bedroom, where Dolly hovered over the bassinet. Bobbie, wrapped in a pink blanket so only her face showed, was still tiny, but a two-pound weight gain had fattened her up so she'd lost her wrinkles and now was as cute as any normal newborn.

"She's still sleeping," Dolly whispered. "Do you think she's all right? Should I wake her up?"

"Let her sleep," Maya advised. "When she's hungry she'll let you know."

She stayed until Bobbie May woke and began to wail. Then she watched Dolly change and feed her, reassuring her whenever she faltered.

"You're doing fine," Maya said when Dolly finished. "You're a natural mother."

Dolly beamed.

Maya turned to the now hovering Pete. "You'd better practice changing her, too. Don't forget, she's your daughter as well as Dolly's."

He shifted his shoulders uneasily. "She's so little."

"Has he held her yet?" Maya asked Dolly.

"He's scared he'll drop her or something," Dolly said.

"Sit down on the couch," Maya told Pete. When he did, Maya reached for the baby and Dolly handed her the pink-wrapped bundle.

For a few minutes Maya admired the baby's bright brown eyes, marveling, as she always did when she held a baby, at the perfection of the tiny hands.

"Curve your left arm to hòld her," Maya said to Pete. He did and she eased Bobbie May into his embrace.

After a moment his apprehensive expression faded into a fascinated smile as he stared down at the baby. "Hey, she didn't start crying," he said. "Maybe she knows it's her papa holding her."

"Babies need to be cuddled by both Mama and Papa," Maya told him. "They need lots of cuddling."

"She's beautiful," Pete said, never taking his eyes from his daughter.

"Yeah," Dolly said. "We're real lucky to have her."

On her way home, Maya stopped at Mrs. Guerrera's for a promised visit. The old woman had been discharged from the Bakersfield hospital last week and Maya hadn't yet been to see her. She found Mrs. Guerrera sitting in the front yard under a large fig tree with embroidery in her lap.

"Me, I feel good," the old woman said. "I don't die easy." She showed Maya what she was working on—a pair of faded blue jeans. "My granddaughter, she asks me to embroider hearts and flowers to wear on her butt. Such days we live in."

"You do beautiful work," Maya said.

Mrs. Guerrera smiled. "Is good you like it. Me, I made you a gift." Reaching into a large wicker basket, she removed a package wrapped in tissue paper and handed it to Maya.

Inside Maya found a pale yellow cotton sheath embroidered with tiny bunches of green and purple grapes hanging from grapevines that twined around the dress from top to bottom. The dress was handmade with exquisite detailing.

"How beautiful!" Maya exclaimed.

Mrs. Guerrera nodded complacently. "For *La Curandera,* nothing is too good."

The old woman's daughter-in-law appeared and insisted Maya have supper with them. Knowing they'd be hurt if she refused, Maya accepted, hoping she could force herself to eat enough to be polite. She had no appetite at all. *La Curandera* had no cure for herself.

As she drove home in the still and hot early evening, Maya's mood, buoyed for a few hours by the visit to Mrs. Guerrera and by seeing Dolly and Pete's baby, sank to a new low.

After entering nursing, she'd held many babies in her arms—boy babies, girl babies, babies of all colors and races. And none of them hers. She'd hold more, but none of them would ever be hers.

The song Joe Halago had played at Sal's housewarming circled endlessly in her head: *Your heart is my heart, one time, no more....* She flicked on her car radio but even the driving beat of the music from the local rock station failed to banish the melancholy words.

She hated to enter her apartment but there was no place else to go. Inside, the whirr of the air conditioner was the only sound and the walls seemed to close around her, imprisoning her. She longed for a way to free herself from the miasma of depression that slowed her movements and clouded her mind. Her grandfather would tell her she needed a cleansing of spirit. A renewal.

"You must reach out with your spirit," she remembered him saying. "You must reach far, reach to all. For all is one. When you understand this, your spirit will be at peace."

Maya sighed. She could go through the motions but, as miserable as she felt, she doubted anything would work. Still, she'd try.

When she got into the car, she found she'd left the embroidered dress on the seat. Perhaps the gift had been made for a purpose she had yet to discover. She wondered if it was meant for her to wear the dress after the cleansing and decided she would.

She drove in the VW until the track grew too rough, then she got out and walked with the dress folded over her arm. The sky was a dark evening blue sprinkled with a few of the brighter stars. The moon hadn't yet risen over the eastern hills. There was still enough light to find her way, enough light to show her the dark clump of sycamores silhouetted against the sky.

She couldn't hear the murmur of Ría Luna. Soon the autumn rains would make the creek rise and set it to gurgling again, but this was the end of summer and the water trickled where it once foamed and splashed.

In a way this was a journey of faith. If she found enough water in Ría Luna to form the pool, she could immerse herself and recite the words her grandfather had taught her, ancient Yaqui words of healing. If there was too little water...

Maya shrugged. At least she'd be no worse off.

Darkness closed around her when she entered the grove, the white trunks of the sycamores like ghosts of trees. She left the scent of dust behind, breathing in a faint dampness. Underfoot the grass was spongy rather than dry and crackling. She'd come into an oasis, a place where magic seemed possible. Although, without Robert, would she ever know magic again?

Night insects chirred intermittently, otherwise silence cloaked the grove. When she reached the creek bank she slipped off her thongs and stepped into the water, relishing the coolness laving her feet. To her dismay the water came no higher than her ankles. She waded downstream to the spot where huge granite boulders trapped the creek water to form the pool.

Laying the embroidered dress on a rock, she removed her shorts, panties and T-shirt and placed them beside the dress. Holding her breath in hope, she eased into the pool.

As she felt the water climb to her thighs, the first ray of moonlight slanted through the sycamore branches to silver the pool. The water was low but there was enough. The pool had survived the drought.

Slowly and carefully she slid the bracelet off her arm and laid the silver snake on her clothes. When she was free of its weight on her arm, a weight in her mind seemed to lift, as well. The bracelet was a symbolic barrier between herself and others, she realized. It kept her apart, no better or worse, but different.

Yet she was no different. She was the same as Laura. As Susan. As Alicia Townsend. In her mind she'd condemned the non-Chicano townspeople in much the same way as she'd believed they scorned her.

I'll be guilty of no more prejudice, she vowed. The bracelet is only a silver ornament, after all. The bracelet is a symbol of healing; it was never meant to close me in and keep others out.

She eased down into the pool until she knelt on the bottom, the water barely covering her breasts. Memories flashed through her mind. Eleven years ago she'd

come here for the first time with Robert, both of them
young, both of them yearning for each other, both of
them foolish. He'd frightened her and she'd fled. But
they'd felt the magic and some of it had clung to them,
refusing to vanish.

She'd come to the moon pool for the second time this
May, newly arrived home again, never suspecting Robert would be drawn to the pool as though by a remnant
of that same magic. Once again he'd startled her and
once again she'd fled from him.

The third time she'd come with Laura and Robert for
a picnic. Laura's presence had diluted the magic hiding
here but hadn't banished it—as both Maya and Robert
had discovered.

And now, the fourth time, she was here. Alone.

Robert rose at dawn following a nearly sleepless night
and, after leaving the house, wandered with no purpose
around the property until, as he passed the manager's
house, Sal hailed him.

"Hey, *compadre*, you want the grand tour, you'll get
it—but how about coffee first?"

Robert wasn't hungry but he drank the mug of coffee
Sal poured for him, the two of them sitting in the courtyard. Overhead, on a tree branch, a mockingbird
chirped and twittered, flicking its white tail feathers.
Instead of cheering him, the bird's song reminded Robert of another bird, the one that sang on the night he'd
made love to Maya on the hill behind the orange grove.

He set the empty coffee mug onto the brick coping
around a pepper tree. Why did everything remind him of
her?

"Rain maybe next week," Sal said. "Ought to get the
raisins covered before it comes."

Robert forced himself to pay attention and an old memory surfaced unexpectedly. "My father worried every year about those damn raisins drying and yet I don't recall any raisin crop that was totally ruined."

Sal grinned. "It's the worrying that prevents the ruin."

"I might have known you'd stand up for my father."

Sal's smile disappeared. "Don't you think I'd do the same for you when you deserve it?"

"Oh hell, forget it," Robert muttered.

"I wouldn't be manager today if your father hadn't taught me everything he knew," Sal said. "He taught me, I taught you. And he knew it. He wanted you to learn but he realized you wouldn't let him teach you one damn thing so he worked through me. He loved you but you couldn't see it. Or wouldn't."

Robert made an inarticulate sound of protest.

"Okay, enough preaching," Sal agreed. "Come on, let's take that tour."

Convinced he had nothing better to do and not wanting to be alone, Robert went along. To distract himself from the aching sense of loss that clung to him like spider silk, he did his best to concentrate on Sal's comments about vines, sprinklers, irrigation lines, leaf rollers and all the other details of the vineyards.

To his surprise, he grew interested enough to begin asking questions and he finally came to the conclusion that he'd gotten rid of Fairfax in the nick of time. Fairfax had been coasting, refusing to buy new equipment so he could make himself look good by keeping down expenses.

Hell, Robert thought as they walked beside the long rows of grapevines, even as half-assed a rancher as me knows equipment breaking down at the wrong time can ruin the year's crop.

He hated to think of the problems that would have arisen if he hadn't taken enough of an interest to fire the man and appoint Sal, his friend. A friend who cared about Pierson's Pride more than he did.

Pierson's Pride.

He was proud of it, Robert decided, amazed at the admission. Proud he owned it. He and Laura.

"Laura's going to transfer to UC Davis next term," he told Sal, reminded of his midnight conversation with his sister. "She says she's going to major in some branch of agriculture."

"She knows a lot about agriculture already," Sal said.

Sal's impassive face told Robert nothing. There was no indication of how Sal felt about Laura being able to achieve a dream that had once been his.

"She's got it in her head to come back and run the vineyards after she graduates," Robert added.

Sal smiled slightly. "More power to her."

"You really think she could?"

"Sure. She's a Pierson, isn't she?"

So am I, Robert thought.

"Piersons know where they belong," Sal added.

Robert blinked. Did he belong here? He'd fought against it most of his life. What if he'd been wrong? Actually, hadn't he been fighting his father rather than Pierson's Pride?

He'd always viewed his father unfavorably—through his mother's eyes. But Sal and Maya, the two people he trusted most, had loved his father. What had George Pierson really been like? Now it was too late for him to discover the truth. But he found himself willing to grant that George had been a man and, like most men, neither all saint nor all sinner.

"I wish I'd known my father better," he said haltingly.

"I wish you had, too," Sal said.

They walked on in silence while Robert struggled to cope with the implications of what he'd just admitted to himself. If his father hadn't been perfect, neither was his mother. If she hadn't let her bitterness over Estella Gabaldon get the upper hand, was it possible the relationship between his father and mother might have been warmer?

"Damn all prejudice!" he exclaimed.

Sal raised his eyebrows but didn't ask for an explanation.

"What's wrong with being a Gabaldon?" Robert demanded. "Gabaldons are no better or worse than Piersons. If my father had married Estella—"

"Chances are you'd never have been born," Sal finished.

Robert smiled sheepishly. "There's truth in that."

"So, okay, are you ready to tell me what's bugging you?" Sal asked.

"I feel like hell."

"You're the doctor but I'll give *my* diagnosis—Something's gone wrong between you and Maya."

Who could he talk to, if not Sal? "I asked her to come to San Francisco with me and she turned me down. Said she couldn't leave the clinic." Robert smiled bitterly. "I don't think it's the clinic keeping her here as much as it's Joe Halago she doesn't want to leave."

Sal snorted. "You go eight years to college and medical school, you intern, you spend more years specializing in internal medicine and you still don't know when a woman's in love with you?''

"If she loved me she'd come to San Francisco with me.''

"*Mi amigo,* you couldn't be more wrong. Believe me, she loves you. But remember, her grandfather was Caesar Gabaldon and he raised her. She grew up understanding she'd inherited an obligation to all of us, the same obligation old Caesar had. How can you expect her to deny a part of herself?''

"You're talking about this *La Curandera* stuff."

"Don't think that's just a nickname. It has meaning for Chicanos. For her." Sal eyed him levelly. "You say Maya doesn't love you. She does. But I don't recall you telling me you love her."

Robert stared at him. *Love.* The very word was terrifying. "I don't know," he said finally. "All I can say is without her I'm lost. Nothing matters."

Sal nodded. "Ever tell her you love her?"

Robert shook his head. "I don't lie to Maya."

"Listen to your own words—without her nothing matters. You're lost. What the hell do you think love is?''

"I wish I knew."

Sal threw up his hands. "I give up. But not before you get to hear my final words of wisdom. Take it from me, Maya's not interested in Doc Halago. He's got a yen for her but he's been careful not to come on to her too strong because he knows about you and Maya and you're his friend. That's how it stands now. I'll be honest—once you go back to the city, who knows? Could be Maya thinks as *loco* as you, thinks that if you can leave her, you don't love her."

Robert's beeper went off—an emergency call from the hospital. He left Sal to hurry to his car but Sal's last words came with him.

The emergency involved a multiple accident call to all the local doctors. A van had rammed a bus on the highway. The injuries kept Robert busy until late in the afternoon. He returned home exhausted, sank onto the side-porch couch and fell asleep.

His mother woke him at seven to eat. He showered and changed, managed a salad and a few bites of steak and returned to the porch, where, after a time, his mother joined him.

"I'm not sure I did the right thing by allowing Laura to drive her convertible back to school," she said.

"Laura's growing up," he assured her. "She'll be all right."

Susan sighed. "I hope so. Did you know she took that ridiculous doll that she calls Don Quixote with her?"

Robert repeated Sal's words. "She earned it."

Susan lapsed into a silence that didn't last long. "You didn't say much at supper. I heard about the accident on the news. How bad was it?"

Robert grimaced. "The only good thing was that all of us worked together doing what we could."

"The doctors, you mean."

He nodded.

"They'll come around," Susan said. "You just wait and see."

Exactly what Maya had told him. He took a deep breath, wishing he could somehow shut Maya out of his mind.

"You seem restless, dear," Susan said. "Why don't you take a walk? I believe the moon's near full so the night should be quite lovely."

The moon's rim showed above the hills when he left the house. What he wanted to do was get in his car and drive to Maya's apartment but he shook his head. They'd only quarrel again. He began to walk aimlessly, with no destination in mind.

He and Joe had worked for more than an hour trying to save a man who'd had a massive coronary following the accident. They'd failed.

"I hate to lose a patient," Joe had said afterward. "Maybe someday I'll learn not to take it so personally when I fail."

Joe's words had reminded him of why Joe was his friend. He liked Joe, as a doctor and as a man. Yet he was deserting Joe just as surely as he was deserting Maya. Joe wasn't physically ready to go back to work full-time—not with the staggering patient load at the clinic, plus being on call all the time.

He'd been feeling sorry for Bill, his San Francisco partner working alone in the city, but Bill's load was nothing compared to what Joe's would be. Besides, Gene Fowler was with Bill now to help handle the city practice.

A realization came to him so suddenly it was as though invisible lightning had pierced his skull, illuminating his mind. *He not only didn't have to return to his San Francisco practice, he didn't want to.*

He wanted to stay in Thompsonville and help Joe at the clinic. He could set up a practice on the side and get along very well. Especially if he lived at home. It *was* his home, after all.

He wanted to be with Maya. Here. In Thompsonville. In his house. He wanted her for keeps. How could he insure that?

Marriage was for keeps.

Marriage!

Well, why not? If you can't live without a woman the only reasonable solution is to marry her so you don't have to live without her.

He loved her. Loving Maya was not repeating his father's mistake—letting her go would be the gravest mistake of his life.

He hoped to God Sal was right about her loving him. What if she'd gotten fed up with his stupidity and blindness and decided Piersons weren't good enough for Gabaldons or Najeros? That he wasn't good enough for her?

Would she marry him? He had to know. Now.

Robert stopped, glancing around, wondering where he was. He found that without intending to, not consciously, he was approaching the sycamore grove.

There was no scent of orange blossoms tonight, no promise of spring. It was autumn, with nothing but winter ahead.

No frogs called tonight, either. Quite likely the stream had dried up completely. There was nothing but bitter memories waiting in the sycamore grove. Robert turned to go back, then stopped, listening.

Was that a faint splash?

He plunged into the grove, running through the darkness under the trees, stumbling, half-falling, rising to run on.

"Maya!" he called, over and over.

He stopped short of the pool. She was there! There in the water, cloaked in moonlight, waiting. For him. He flung off his clothes, impatient to join her. But when he came to the edge of the pool he paused.

"Maya," he said softly. "Maya, I love you."

She rose to her feet, water droplets gleaming, silvering her beauty. As she reached her arms toward him, she smiled and his heart turned over.

He splashed into the pool and took her hands, looking into her eyes. Now he understood why she'd once told him she wouldn't go into the pool with him. "Unless—" she'd said, and then refused to finish the sentence.

He was certain he knew what she hadn't said. *Unless we are pledging ourselves, one to the other.*

The moon pool was a symbol of their love. He'd loved her eleven years ago and denied it. He'd never deny his love for her again.

"Marry me, Maya," he whispered. "Marry me and live with me at Pierson's Pride?"

She gazed at him for a long, tension-filled moment before she spoke.

"Yes. Yes, I will. I love you, Robert. I always have." Her soft affirmation throbbed through him.

Slowly, reverently, he drew her to him. And then she was in his arms, fitted against him as only Maya had ever fitted, her warm lips welcoming, setting him ablaze with her response.

He wanted to tell her all the painful lessons he'd had to learn to reconcile the past, all the decisions he'd struggled to reach to insure a future that was right for both of them, but the necessary words had been said— all others could wait. She'd agreed to marry him; nothing else mattered.

Nothing except their pledge to one another in this place where they'd failed themselves and each other so long ago. A wordless pledge, an act of love.

In the moonlight, in the shallows of the pool, they came together, and in the wonder of her embrace it seemed to him that they made love for the very first time.

A piercing delight filled Maya as they joined, a feeling above and beyond the searing passion Robert always evoked in her. Under the moon, with the water lapping gently around them, they'd discovered the secret of the pool.

Loving him was right, was meant to be. He loved her in return and this was the magic they would always bring to each other.

Chapter Sixteen

Maya, her white veil pushed back over her antique headpiece, glanced around the crowded room as she listened absently to a guest reminiscing about her own long-ago wedding. All her friends were there, not only from Thompsonville but from San Diego, as well. Sal, she noted, seemed interested in Danielle Markovich, who'd been in her nursing class.

Sal looked elegant in the tux he'd worn as best man but no male in the room came close to being as magnificent as the groom. Robert wore his formal gear with the same ease as he did shorts and T-shirt. He always dominated his clothes. She watched him as he talked to one of the ushers—a friend of his from Stanford—and smiled to herself. He looked so relieved.

Robert had sailed through the week before the wedding with no obvious nervousness. He'd been Dr. Cool in person until the rehearsal jitters hit him. After that he'd been so nervous that Maya had worried more about him than her own anxieties. Not until Sal, taking the traditional role of the father, had marched with her up the aisle and handed her over to the groom had Robert seemed to relax.

She'd remember the beauty of their wedding as long as she lived.

Laura drifted past in animated conversation with another usher friend of Robert's, the teal blue Maya had chosen for the bridesmaids complementing her fair coloring.

". . . and after all that," the guest, a friend of Susan's named Henderson, said, "would you believe that it rained on our wedding?"

Maya shook her head. "What a shame."

"It was in July," Mrs. Henderson went on. "It never rains in July in the Valley. Here you are getting married in December when it ought to rain and you have a beautiful day. You're lucky!"

She *was* lucky, Maya thought. She and Robert both. They'd persisted against the odds and come up winners.

"I imagine it was Susan who insisted on having the reception at the house," Mrs. Henderson probed. "She's very persuasive."

"She's been extremely helpful," Maya said noncommittally.

Susan's quiet acceptance once Robert announced wedding plans had surprised him as much as it had Maya. In their initial confusion over her reaction, Susan had found her chance to take control of the event and, except for details, she'd planned the wedding and the reception.

"Mom's happy 'cause she got her way after all," Laura had pointed out to Maya. "Like, your marriage brings Robert back to Pierson's Pride."

Apparently even Maya Gabaldon Najero was acceptable to Susan under those circumstances!

At least I chose my own gown, Maya thought ruefully, wondering if Susan had resigned herself to the marriage as early as the day of the benefit fair at the grape festival. In that case, Susan's "I'm sure we'll get along together very well" would make lots more sense than it seemed to at the time.

Of course that would mean Susan predicted Robert's proposal and Maya's acceptance before the fact....

Mrs. Henderson picked that moment to comment on the gown. "So unusual. And so very beautiful with all that hand detail."

Mrs. Guerrera and her daughter-in-law had made a more elaborate copy of Estella Gabaldon's Mexican wedding dress, the dress Estella had never worn. Maya's headpiece came from the Pierson side. All the brides since Robert's great-grandmother had worn it.

"May you be happy," Susan had said when she placed it on Maya's head before the wedding. Coming from her, the words had brought a lump to Maya's throat.

"Mrs. Henderson," Robert said as he slid an arm around Maya's waist. "How nice to see you."

She wagged a finger at him. "You were a naughty boy not to come visit me when you lived in San Francisco. Instead, I had to drive all the way down here to see you. But, since it's your wedding day and you've chosen such a lovely bride, I'll forgive you."

Robert smiled at Mrs. Henderson. "Thank you."

Other well-wishers came up and she moved on.

"I'll be glad when all this is over," Robert whispered a few minutes later into Maya's ear. "Some sadist invented wedding receptions—it's cruel and unusual punishment when a man has to go through torture to get married and then can't even be alone with his wife."

She slanted him a reproving glance. "Torture?"

He hugged her against his side. "Okay, so I admit the ceremony moved me. But I refuse to believe you're enjoying this any more than I am." He waved his hand at the wedding guests and the caterers with trays—almost everyone in motion, many talking, some laughing.

"I don't mind. After all, I've never been married before."

"And you won't be again," he assured her. "After surviving this, I'm never letting you go."

She tipped her head to look past the veil and smile at him. He leaned down and brushed his lips across hers. "Let's at least go onto the patio," he murmured. "There's not as many out there."

With his arm at her waist, he led her through the French doors. The sun was warm and the sky clear, though the air had a cool undertone. Robert guided her toward the canopied garden swing at the far end but they found another couple sitting there so he turned back.

"I remember the party here," she said. "I watched Julie Symond kiss you and positively seethed with jealousy."

"You should talk! Who was it I saw cozying up to some musician she went to high school with?"

Reminded of how the party ended with Laura running off to Sal, Maya said, "Laura seems more mature since she's left home."

"I think she's grown a tad wiser. But that doesn't mean she's given up."

Maya stared at him. "What do you mean?"

"Why do you think she's going to transfer to Davis in January?"

"That's obvious. Laura's half-owner of Pierson's Pride and she's serious about her responsibility. She wants to take a hand in running the vineyards once she graduates."

"Sure, but that's only the surface reason. The hidden agenda is still Sal. Piersons get an idea fixed in their heads and can't get rid of it." He traced the curve of her upper lip with his forefinger. "I tried to get rid of you for eleven years. What good did it do me?" He spun her around, her veil floating in the cool breeze. "Just look what happened."

"Are you sorry?" she asked, gazing at him through her lashes.

In answer, he kissed her—more thoroughly this time. He broke the embrace when several guests began applauding. "It's past time for us to leave," he muttered.

"I can't go without throwing my bouquet," she reminded him.

"Then let's go in and get that over with."

Hand in hand, they walked toward the French doors. As they stepped through Maya overheard Susan speaking to several of her friends.

"Maya has succeeded in bringing Robbie back to the land, where he belongs," Susan said. "Nothing pleases me more than to have them move into this house."

"But what about you?" a woman asked. "Won't it be hard with two women—"

"Oh, my dear, I thought you knew," Susan said. "I'm moving into Robbie's condo in San Francisco. I've always loved the city—I have so many friends there. But my secret ambition is to update my art history degree and dabble in gallery or museum work.''

''Won't you miss Pierson's Pride?'' another woman asked.

''Not terribly. Remember, I'm not a Pierson by birth. I always felt it was my husband's more than mine. Of course I'll be back to visit—especially after the grand-children arrive.''

The women laughed and Susan glanced toward Robert and Maya with a sly smile.

They looked at each other and his arm slid around Maya's waist to draw her against his side. They hadn't discussed children but the glow she saw in his eyes reflected her own deep feelings.

Selfish or not, Susan had a strange habit of being right. Pierson's Pride needed the laughter of children to sweep away the years of sadness, children who were happy because they were loved. Their children, a mixture of Gabaldon and Pierson.

Whatever her reasons, Susan had also begun a project they must go on with. They had a duty to persuade those townspeople who were better off that they had an obligation to those less fortunate. La Raza Clínica was a good place to begin. Progress was always slow—a little at a time. Maya never would have believed it possible six months ago but perhaps someday the chasm between the Anglo and the Chicano in Thompsonville could be bridged by goodwill on both sides.

She started to share her thoughts with Robert but he shook his head. ''Tell me later, when we're alone. After the bouquet tossing. And maybe after a few other things.''

The warmth in Robert's gaze kindled an impatience in her, an eagerness to be alone with him. It seemed an eternity before the bridesmaids gathered at the foot of the front steps and the photographer found the focus he wanted. Maya lifted her bouquet of orange blossoms and tossed it high above their heads. Hands reached, voices squealed.

"I got it!" Laura shrieked jubilantly. She jumped up and down waving the bouquet. "*Muchas gracias,* Maya."

Maya smiled and waved, waiting for them to clear a path so she and Robert could hurry down the stairs to the waiting limo. From her vantage point, she saw who the best man was staring at and caught his fleeting emotion before his expression went blank.

Laura, her cheeks pink, stared back at Sal, making no effort to hide what she felt.

Maya glanced at Robert and saw that he'd also witnessed the byplay.

"I told you," he said.

"But I didn't know Sal felt the same way toward Laura," she protested. "He's kept it well hidden."

"He's trying to protect her." Robert shook his head. "Little does he know he's the one who needs protection. She'll never change her mind." He shrugged. "Actually, I've been thinking of offering Sal a part interest in the vineyards anyway. He deserves it. What do you think the chances are that Laura will agree?"

"I think that in ten years the place is going to be overrun with kids," Maya said.

"Yours and mine—and maybe his and hers. Right." Robert grinned and offered his arm. She took it and they ran down the stairs, rice pelting them from all sides until they reached the limo.

"If I'd been a tad wiser we could have done this eleven years ago," he said as he slid into the back seat beside her.

"You know what my grandfather would have said to that?" she asked solemnly.

"El Curandero Gabaldon?" Robert frowned, seemingly a bit dismayed. "I can't imagine."

"Mejor tarde que nunca." She deepened her voice, making each word sound as portentous as possible.

He laughed and pulled her into his arms. "What a wise grandfather you had. I agree completely with old Caesar—better late than never."

* * * * *

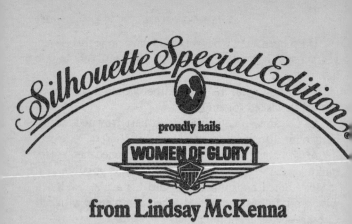

Silhouette Special Edition

proudly hails

WOMEN OF GLORY

from Lindsay McKenna

Soar with Dana Coulter, Molly Rutledge and Maggie Donovan—Lindsay McKenna's WOMEN OF GLORY. On land, sea or air, these three Annapolis grads challenge danger head-on, risking life and limb for the glory of their country—and for the men they love!

May: NO QUARTER GIVEN (SE #667) Dana Coulter is on the brink of achieving her lifelong dream of flying—and of meeting the man who would love to take her to new heights!

June: THE GAUNTLET (SE #673) Molly Rutledge is determined to excel on her own merit, but Captain Cameron Sinclair is equally determined to take gentle Molly under his wing....

July: UNDER FIRE (SE #679) Indomitable Maggie never thought her career—or her heart—would come under fire. But all that changes when she teams up with Lieutenant Wes Bishop!

SEWG-1

Bestselling author **NORA ROBERTS** captures all the romance, adventure, passion and excitement of Silhouette in a special miniseries.

THE CALHOUN WOMEN

Four charming, beautiful and fiercely independent sisters set out on a search for a missing family heirloom—an emerald necklace—and each finds something even more precious . . . passionate romance.

Look for THE CALHOUN WOMEN miniseries starting in June.

CALWOM-1

Silhouette Books®

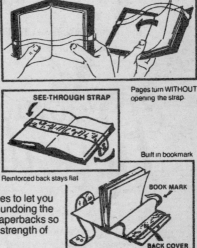

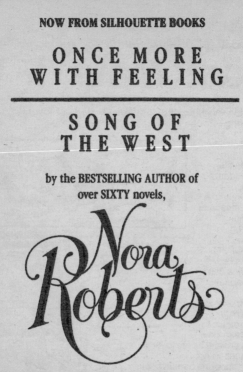
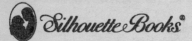